The Seafaring Rogue

Pirates of Britannia

SKY PURINGTON

D1518367

Cover Design by Kim Killion @ The Killion Group, Inc.
Edited by *Cathy McElhaney*

The Pirates of Britannia World

Savage of the Sea
by Eliza Knight

Leader of Titans
by Kathryn Le Veque

The Sea Devil
by Eliza Knight

Sea Wolfe
by Kathryn Le Veque

The Sea Lyon
by Hildie McQueen

The Blood Reaver
by Barbara Devlin

Plunder by Knight
by Mia Pride

The Seafaring Rogue
by Sky Purington

Stolen by Starlight
by Avril Borthiry

The Ravishing Rees
by Rosamund Winchester

The Marauder
by Anna Markland

The Pirate's Temptation
by Tara Kingston

Pearls of Fire
by Meara Platt

The Righteous Side of Wicked
by Jennifer Bray-Weber

Table of Contents

About the Book

Left for dead on the shores of Scotland, Fraser MacLomain falls in love with the healer who saves him. Yet Elspeth MacLauchlin has deep dark secrets. Hidden truths rooted in a century old family feud. A vendetta that is soon resurrected by vicious enemies who steal her away during a late night pirate attack.

Bent on saving her and reaping revenge, Fraser embraces a life of piracy. Cutthroat, out for blood, he relentlessly pursues his nemesis long after rumor has Elspeth dead. Long after he abandons love for bitterness. But even a hardened heart can be thawed, as he soon discovers when catching his foe begins a high seas adventure ripe with passion, intrigue, and treasure.

Legend of the Pirates of Britannia

I N THE YEAR of our Lord 854, a wee lad by the name of Arthur MacAlpin set out on an adventure that would turn the tides of his fortune, for what could be more exciting than being feared and showered with gold?

Arthur wanted to be king. A sovereign as great as King Arthur, who came hundreds of years before him. The legendary knight who was able to pull a magical sword from stone, met ladies in lakes and vanquished evil with a vast following who worshipped him. But while that King Arthur brought to mind dreamlike images of a roundtable surrounded by chivalrous knights and the ladies they romanced, MacAlpin wanted to summon night terrors from every babe, woman and man.

Aye, MacAlpin, king of the pirates of Britannia would be a name most feared. A name that crossed children's lips when the candles were blown out at night. When a shadow passed over a wall, was it the pirate king? When a ship sailed into port in the dark hours of night, was it him?

As the fourth son of the conquering Pictish King Cináed, Arthur wanted to prove himself to his father. He wanted to make his father proud, and show him that he, too, could be a conqueror. King Cináed was praised widely for having run off the Vikings, for saving his people, for amassing a vast and strong army. No one would dare encroach on his conquered lands when they would have to face the end of his blade.

Arthur wanted that, too. He wanted to be feared. Awed. To hold his sword up and have devils come flying from the tip.

So, it was on a fateful summer night in 854 that, at the age of ten and nine, Arthur amassed a crew of young and roguish Picts and stealthily commandeered one of his father's ships. They blackened the sails to hide them from those on watch and began an adventure that would last a lifetime and beyond.

The lads trolled the seas, boarding ships and sacking small coastal villages. In fact, they even sailed so far north as to raid a Viking village in the name of his father. By the time they returned to Oban, and the seat of King Cináed, all of Scotland was raging about Arthur's atrocities. Confused, he tried to explain, but his father would not listen and would not allow him back into the castle.

King Cináed banished his youngest son from the land, condemned his acts as evil and told him he never wanted to see him again.

Enraged and experiencing an underlying layer of mortification, Arthur took to the seas, gathering men as he went, and building a family he could trust that would not shun him. They ravaged the sea as well as the land—using his clan's name as a lasting insult to his father for turning him out.

The legendary Pirate King was rumored to be merciless, the type of vengeful pirate who would drown a babe in his mother's own milk if she didn't give him the pearls at her neck. But with most rumors, they were mostly steeped in falsehoods meant to intimidate. In fact, there may have been a wee boy or two he saved from an untimely fate. Whenever they came across a lad or lass in need, as Arthur himself had once been, they took them into the fold.

One ship became two. And then three, four, five, until a score of ships with blackened sails roamed the seas.

These were his warriors. A legion of men who adored him, respected him, followed him, and, together, they wreaked havoc on the blood ties that had sent him away. And generations upon generations, country upon country, they would spread far and wide until people feared them from horizon to horizon. Every pirate king to follow would be named MacAlpin, so his father's banishment would never be forgotten.

Forever lords of the sea. A daring brotherhood, where honor among thieves reigns supreme, and crushing their enemies is a thrilling pastime.

These are the pirates of Britannia, and here are their stories....

Was not the sea

Made for the Free,

Land for courts and chains alone?

Here we are slaves,

But, on the waves,

Love and Liberty's all our own.

No eye to watch, and no tongue to wound us

All earth forgot, and all heaven around us –

Then come o'er the sea,

Maiden, with me,

Mine through sunshine, storms, and snows

Seasons may roll,

But the true soul

Burns the same, where'er it goes.

–Thomas Moore

Prologue

Province of Mearns, Scotland
Stonehaven Bay
1448

H E CRACKED OPEN an eye only to squeeze it shut against the blinding sun. His mouth was bone dry, his tongue swollen and his parched lips caked with salt.

Where was he?

What happened?

He tried to wiggle his fingers and toes but felt nothing.

Was he dead?

Was this hell?

His mind was blank. Empty.

Who *was* he?

Awareness came and went, and with it sounds. Waves crashed in the distance. Seagulls cried overhead. Brine and seaweed scented the cool wind. He tried to move toward life, toward all he felt around him, but it was impossible.

He was too far gone.

Or so he thought until a wracking cough gripped him and a sharp pain lanced his mid-section.

"Shh," came a gentle feminine voice from far away. "Dinnae move quite yet."

When a soft hand touched his forehead, he realized that she was, in fact, right beside him. He attempted to open his eyes again, but it was too painful.

"Where am I?" he tried to say, but instead more coughs overcame him and something warm trickled out of the corner of his mouth. Mayhap blood? From what though? He recalled no battle. No skirmish of any sort.

"I'm going to move ye someplace safe and tend to your wounds." She still sounded far away. "But first, a wee drink if ye can."

A drink? Was she mad? While certainly thirsty, he could barely breathe let alone swallow. Nevertheless, moments later he felt her tender touch as she tipped his head forward ever-so-slightly and something bitter slid down his throat.

He flinched and tried to speak again, but it was no use.

Everything drifted further and further away.

He tried to stay with her, wanted to hold on, but he started to slip into a deep dark abyss. He had no choice but to give in and allow Fate to have him. To follow a path that might very well end in death.

Or—as he hoped before he faded altogether—a path that might just lead back to her.

Chapter One

A Fortnight Later

NIGHTMARES CAME AND went. Murky, echoing places full of black shadows and evil warnings. Yet still, there were kinder voices eager to tell him something. Remind him. Memories just out of reach. Truths being hidden. But he never heard them clearly.

He only heard her.

The lass by the shore.

Like an angel, her gentle voice floated in and out of the dark places in his mind, pulling him back from a bottomless chasm. He felt her comforting touch. Her healing hands. Though there were bouts of physical pain, they lessened. Rather, he began to welcome the moments of discomfort because he knew she would be touching him again.

It was during one of those times that he finally broke free from the hazy, otherworldly place he had been in, and opened his eyes. Not much. Just a mere slit so he could watch her.

Not surprisingly, her appearance was as bonny as her voice. She had rich auburn tinted dark brown hair and delicate, even features. Her lips were full and plush and her long, thick lashes, a shade darker than her hair. Lending character to her startling beauty, a light smattering of freckles dusted her cheekbones and nose.

It was her eyes, however, that made it impossible to look away. A sparkling, pale copper, they were undoubtedly the sort of eyes that could hold a lad prisoner and melt his heart.

"Good morn," she said softly, evidently aware he had awoken as she finished with the wrap on his stomach then lifted a skin of water to his mouth. "Dinnae try to speak but drink some water, aye? Ye need to regain your strength."

He did as she asked, relishing the cool liquid. More so, the poignant feeling he experienced the moment her eyes finally met his. Did he know her from somewhere? Had they met before? She seemed so familiar. So important.

"Thank ye," he managed to whisper as she settled his head back.

She nodded and was about to say something when a tall, dark haired man entered and scowled in his direction. "Is he awake then?"

Only then did he take stock of his surroundings.

They were in a relatively small cave with a crackling fire. Based on the whistling wind and the sound of waves, they remained close to the shore. Bushels of fresh herbs hung about so he would say they were close to woodland as well. A young, slender lad mayhap around thirteen winters sat quietly in the corner grinding something in a small wooden bowl.

The man who had just entered was a rough sort with brown hair and a braided beard. He wore black boots, a plaid with faded colors and a brown bandana wrapped around his head. Most notable though were the variety of weapons tucked here and there. He was a fighter. And based on his liquid movements a good one.

"Aye, he's awake," she replied to the bearded man before her eyes returned to him. "Have ye a name then?"

"Not that I remember," he said hoarsely, welcoming more water.

"Aye then," she murmured. "Ye took a serious hit to the head, but hopefully it will come back to ye." She gestured in the stranger's direction. "That's my brother Douglas MacLauchlin, and my name's Elspeth."

"Elspeth MacLauchlin," he whispered, as something occurred to him. "I knew your lot at one time."

Though she offered a small smile, the look in her eyes was telling.

"Ye dinnae remember me though, aye?" he murmured, flinching from a twinge of pain as she propped a blanket behind him and helped him sit up against the wall.

"Nay, I'm afraid not." She shook her head as she made sure he was comfortable then tucked a plaid around him more securely. That's when he realized he wore no clothing. "Ye arenae familiar to any of us."

He nodded, disappointed. It was frustrating not knowing who he was. Having no sense of identity.

He eyed Douglas' unusual clothing, trying to place it. "Where am I then?"

"You're in a cave near my village." Her eyes flickered from Douglas back to him as she removed the meat that had been roasting on a spit. "'Tis safer here for now."

"And where is your village?" he asked.

When she told him, he nodded. "I know of the area." He met their surprised looks with one of his own as certain things came flooding back. "For that matter, I remember Scotland quite well." He shook his head. "Though I dinnae think I'm from around here."

In fact, he was positive he was not.

His eyes fell to the bandage wrapped around his waist then returned to Elspeth. "Thank ye for seeing to me, lass."

"Aye then," another man declared as he entered. "Our good Elspeth brought ye back from the brink of death, she did." He grinned and nodded his way. "The name's Innis."

He greeted him in kind, taking note of his size and attire as well. Though not as tall as Douglas, his shoulders were broader and his muscles more substantial. His flaming red hair was long and wild with plenty of small braids interwoven. Like Elspeth's brother, he wore a bandana around his head but breeches instead of a plaid.

After Douglas caught him up, Innis shook his head. "So ye dinnae recall your name, aye? Ye poor bastard." He grinned as he tossed him a skin. "Ye'll be needing that then, I'd say."

He nodded, grateful as he took a swig of what turned out to be whisky. It was clear Innis was a lighthearted if not boisterous soul.

"Thank ye, lass," he murmured, his attention no longer on Innis but Elspeth as she handed him a wooden plate with rabbit. "For everything."

She nodded then urged the others to eat before she turned her attention his way again. "I was not the only one who took care of ye." She nodded in the direction of the quiet lad. "My apprentice Audric did as well. He helped me get ye here then saw to your more personal needs."

He arched his brows at that, grateful he supposed all things considered.

When he nodded at the boy, Audric murmured, "*Bonjour.*" His eyes flickered nervously to the other men before they returned to the safety of whatever he was grinding.

Speaking French, Elspeth murmured something reassuring to Audric before her eyes returned to his.

"Ye must truly have God on your side." She watched him curiously. "Ye took verra well to our administrations and healed quickly considering ye fought the fever for so long." Her eyes fell to his abdomen. "Though ye still feel some pain, your injuries should not give ye issue for much longer. 'Tis a miracle really."

"Och, aye!" Innis appeared properly mystified as he kept grinning. "I'd say he's got ancient druid blood in him. 'Tis said they possessed mystical healing qualities."

"Ye and your stories." Douglas snorted and perked an exasperated brow at Innis. "This one will be about a druid of centuries past washing up on our shores then, aye?"

"Mayhap." Innis chuckled. "It doesnae hurt to have a tale to tell the lassies." He looked away from Douglas and winked in his direction. "'Twill give them a good stir and likely in your favor, friend."

Elspeth rolled her eyes. "He needs rest before lasses, Innis."

That was a matter of opinion. Especially with the likes of Elspeth around.

As they ate, he continued listening to the three of them as he discreetly watched her. She had tied the bottom of her dress up in such a fashion that it created breeches of a sort. The edges were wet, and her small feet were dirty so he would guess she had recently walked the shore.

"They're starting to grow suspicious in the village, Sister," Douglas murmured. "Ye should make an appearance more often lest they find what you're hiding in here."

"Aye," Innis agreed.

He couldn't help but notice the interest in Innis' eyes as they followed Elspeth. Though he might claim to enjoy the lasses, one stood out amongst the rest. She, in turn, didn't seem to notice that she caught anyone's eye. But then he got the impression she wasn't all that concerned with what men thought of her. She was an independent sort if ever there was one.

"They'll say what they'll say then." She shook her head and cinched her hair back into a sloppy knot. "I've neither the time nor inclination to worry over gossip."

"Then ye care nothing for your new patient." Douglas shrugged. "Nor do ye care for Ma and Da and our wee sisters, aye?"

"Och." She sighed then relented. "Now that our new friend's awake,

I'll head back there more often." Her dubious eyes went to him. "Though he will still need to be tended to for a few more days."

"Aye, then," Douglas agreed. "I think 'twould also be good to bring him to the village, so they know what ye've been up to." He frowned. "'Tis not a good thing to keep secrets in these parts and well ye know it."

Something about the tone of his voice made Elspeth still. "What is it then, Brother?" Her eyes flickered between Douglas and Innis. "What are ye not saying?"

Troubled, the men eyed each other before Douglas finally spoke.

"Rumors have reached the Spanish pirates, Sister." His eyes darkened. "Rumors that should have remained folklore."

"Folklore that should have remained a secret," Innis added, his steady eyes on Elspeth.

Their gazes held for a moment before she spoke. "How many allies have ye in Cruden Bay?"

"Enough." Douglas' distrustful eyes slid his way again. "But an ally can quickly become an enemy when there is rumor of loot, aye?" He popped some meat in his mouth and spoke around his food. "The only true allies we have in the area are the *Devils of the Deep*."

So trouble was afoot.

Though unfamiliar with them, that name was telling. While he might have been a bit off his game when he awoke, he understood their strange clothing now. These men were pirates in league, naturally, with even more pirates. Yet what big secret did they keep?

His attention returned to Elspeth. How was she involved? Because the thought of her in danger made him uneasy. Though tempted to ask her, he focused on the more immediate problem.

"If I go back to the village with ye," he said, "will they not wonder why ye didnae bring me there, to begin with?"

"'Tis not for ye to worry over," she assured, her eyes not quite meeting his. "If ye are my lad, they willnae overly question it."

"Your lad?" Innis' brows shot up. "Is that not going a wee bit too far, lassie?"

"I dinnae think so." Elspeth shook her head. "Not if what ye say is true." She gave Innis a pointed look. "Just look at him. He might have thinned some from his injuries, but his size tells of a mighty warrior." She cocked her head. "Would it not soothe many to know he's to be kin not merely a stranger passing through? That he could help protect us if unwanted company makes their way here?"

He looked down at himself and realized she was right. There was no need to stand to know he was taller and in better shape than the lot of them. For a brief flash, as he eyed his hand and clenched his fist, he remembered holding a sword. The familiar weight of it. The berserker fury and adrenaline rush he felt as he ran it through another.

Unfortunately, as soon as he recalled it, the memory vanished.

"So ye think to claim this newcomer as your lad and fool them all, aye, lass?" Innis scowled. "Even your sweet ma and da?" He shook his head. "'Tis unwise."

"Actually, 'tis not such a bad idea," Douglas mused as he considered him. It seemed opportunity outweighed wariness for the moment. "What say ye, stranger? Would ye swear yourself to Elspeth until we've done away with the current threat to our people?"

"Aye," he said, more than content acting as though the bonny lass was his. Yet he would not go into this blindly. "Just so long as ye tell me what I'll be facing and what it is I'm protecting outside of your sister and kin."

"I can protect myself," Elspeth muttered under her breath. "This charade is only to give our people peace of mind."

She might say as much, but he would feel better offering his protection.

As he eyed her, he realized with pleasure that interest in him might also be a factor in her quickly hatched plan. Did he not detect breathlessness in her voice when she spoke of them pretending to be together? Was there not a flush to her cheeks when she glanced at him?

"Ye'll be facing savage Spanish pirates and mayhap French scoundrels," Douglas responded in answer to his question. "Ruthless bastards all." Anger shadowed his face as he shook his head. "As to the treasure they seek, 'tis but a handful of stones surrounded by superstition."

"That sounds ominous, indeed," he replied dryly, watching each and every one of them closely. "Yet despite superstition, these stones are desired. 'Tis odd, aye?"

"'Tis as it can be when stories travel from campfire to campfire," Elspeth said softly, her troubled eyes on the flames. "They become grander and grander until they speak of treasure troves that dinnae exist. Bundles of precious gems and sparkling pearls the likes of which ye've never seen."

Based on the way her voice grew throaty, and her pupils flared, this tale had more than a grain of truth to it. If he didn't know better, he would say she embellished very little.

"A myth," she continued in a whisper as she rubbed a small piece of checkered wool between her fingers. "Yet a dangerous one." Her eyes finally turned to his. "One that I fear ye are a part of now."

He knew he was if for no other reason than to keep her safe as she had done for him. And though he told himself he did it because it was the right thing to do, he knew better. He had no desire to leave her in the lurch or otherwise. She intrigued him. Captivated him.

It wasn't just her remarkable beauty and daring eyes, but something else as well.

There was a mystery about her he needed to understand. A complicated past that somehow felt aligned with his. As though Fate had brought them together. He felt it so strongly that he was about to say as much. Yet the thought trailed off as his eyes were drawn to the wool in her hands once more.

The blue and green scrap of plaid.

"'Twas mine," he whispered as he suddenly remembered something very important. "'Twas my clan's." His eyes rose to hers as one small part of his past became very clear. "I remember my name. 'Tis MacLomain…Fraser MacLomain."

Chapter Two

FROM THE MOMENT he had washed up on her shore Elspeth rarely took her eyes off her handsome patient. This moment proved no different. His steady, near inescapable gaze, held her. She could lose herself in those thickly lashed icy pale blue eyes if she were not careful. Eyes that when he first opened them earlier seemed eerily familiar.

As though in another life she might have stared into them countless times.

Then there was his appearance. For all her local travels and caring for the sick, she had never come across a better built man. Broad shouldered and well-muscled, he would likely be very imposing when he finally stood. And his face? Captivating. Intense. With hair as dark as night, he possessed features so well chiseled the gods must envy him.

His was truly a face that could haunt a lass's dreams if she let it.

Battle scars ran across his right shoulder and down his side. Though she had done her best to treat it, she expected several more would remain on his abdomen. By all accounts, they *should* have lost him. In fact, she thought they had several times. But he was very strong, a true survivor, and had struggled through.

Now here he sat with those eyes of his pinning her in place as he sought the truth. Secrets that had long been hers and her kin's. Yet she had a feeling as he seemingly stared straight into her soul, that in the end, she would keep very little from him.

"'Tis nice to meet ye, Fraser MacLomain," she murmured, still rubbing his scrap of tartan absently. "I've heard of your clan."

"Aye?" His brows swept up. "And what have ye heard, lass?"

His voice was deep and tempting. The sort that reminded her it had been far too long since she lay with a man. She cleared her throat and tried to remain focused. Not easy when she knew full well what rested beneath his blanket.

"The MacLomains are verra powerful," Elspeth finally managed. "And as the tales tell it, known for their mystic ways." Her eyes returned to his. "They were also once allied with us MacLauchlin's."

His brows remained arched in curiosity. "The MacLomains are known for their mystic ways?"

"Aye, all sorts of fantastical stories are told about them." She kept a touch of both mystery and disbelief in her voice. "Children's tales about witches and wizards and magic." A wry grin tugged at her mouth. "All folklore of course, but great fun to tell the wee ones on a cold winter's night."

"Yet ye yourself said I healed faster than most," he said softly.

"Och." She chuckled, not about to entertain any more of this nonsense. "'Twas just good medicine." Then, because it was true however breathlessly she spoke it. "Along with such a strong, healthy…fit patient."

She didn't miss the amusement that flickered in his eyes at her stunted yet complimentary words.

"As to our clans." He tilted his head in question. "Are we not allied anymore?"

"Not as we once were," she replied. "Most of us are on the east coast now whilst the MacLomains remain in Argyll."

He nodded. Where she thought for sure he would want to know more about his clan, he remained focused on the subject at hand. "So do these stones your enemies speak of still exist?"

She eyed him for a moment before she came to a decision and looked at Douglas. "If I'm to ask him to protect our lot then I'll give him the truth."

"I dinnae know," Douglas began, but she cut him off.

"He has the right to know, Brother." She shook her head. "And what harm could it do?"

"'Tis yet to be seen," he muttered before he relented, knowing full well she would get her way. "Aye then lassie, do as ye will."

"I will." She notched her chin, daring them to defy her as she looked from Douglas to Innis. "And I'll do it alone. Because soon after he'll need to rest."

Innis' brows slammed together in jealous suspicion. "*Will* he then?"

"Och," she muttered as she took their plates and shoo'd them along, knowing full well what he was implying. "We'll meet ye at the village in a few days, aye?" Her eyes went to Douglas one last time. "Meanwhile, if ye can rally additional support as well as gather more information about the upcoming threat, 'twould not be a bad idea."

"Aye, lass," he grumbled as his eyes narrowed on Fraser one last time. A warning that he remain on his best behavior. Then he shook his head and said something under his breath that sounded a lot like he was a captain now and knew what should be done. Naturally, she ignored him knowing full well he appreciated her feedback.

She smiled warmly at Audric and asked him for privacy as well. Always mindful and polite, he complied. Though his family had paid good coin for his education, she would have taught him for free. Not only was he kindhearted, but he had a natural talent with herbs and a soothing bedside manner that put patients at ease.

Speaking of patients.

Fraser's disarming eyes never left her as she grabbed a small pouch and then sat down beside him. She and her kin had never shared this tale with friends let alone a stranger so how it reached Spanish ears was a mystery. Yet it had, and that meant very bad things were coming their way. The sort of danger that meant she would need a man of Fraser's caliber watching over her kin.

Some, including her brother, might say she didn't know him nearly well enough to put her faith in him. But her gut told her otherwise. He was a much better sort than those Douglas and Innis consorted with. He wasn't a ruthless demon set to destroy all in his path. If anything, he was a protector. An honorable man.

So she would tell him their story.

"Nearly a century ago, my great-grandfather turned the tables on a raiding ship," she began. "Rumor had it they were Spaniards. Others said they were French. Either way, he caught wind that they were coming and took them unaware." She shook her head. "Determined to make an example of what it meant to attack his beloved castle, he killed them all and kept what treasure was already aboard."

"And that wasnae the wisest move, aye?" he murmured.

"Nay, 'twas not." She sighed. "But then it seems my great-grandfather tended to think beyond his means and didnae fear repercussions. He thought his actions would frighten away any that dared defy him again." She clenched her jaw, angered by his foolhardy actions. "What he didnae take into consideration was that the sort he dealt with would not fear but learn from his actions."

"Ah," Fraser said softly. "So more came."

"Aye, they came," she replied. "This time with far more men, weapons, and stealth." She narrowed her eyes, envisioning her ancestors' doomed castle. "Searching for stolen treasure and retribution, they came in the dead of night and slaughtered nearly everyone. Then they looted the castle before burning it to the ground."

Fraser remained respectfully silent as she continued.

"Only a handful of people escaped including my great-grandmother with her son, my grandfather," she said, not woeful in the least as she continued. "My great-grandfather was captured and tortured in hopes that he might tell them where he hid the treasure. And he did. Or so they thought. As it turned out he taunted them into killing him before they verified his confession." She shook her head again. "Which, it seems, was untrue."

"So the treasure was never found?" Fraser said.

"Nay, nor was there any record of survivors," she replied. "My great-grandmother was strong and wise in the ways of survival. She changed our surname and made her way across Scotland to begin a new life." Her eyes went to his. "To this day we only use the MacLauchlin name amongst our immediate kin lest we draw unwanted attention."

"Yet ye shared with me," he murmured, his assessment quick and astute. "Because this tale has been resurrected and rumor tells of MacLauchlin's being here."

"Aye, not just that but a treasure map of sorts." She poured small flat stones out of the pouch and held them in her open palm. "These are all that remain to show us where the treasure was hidden." She pointed out the various slashes on each stone. "When put together in a certain order from a precise location, they will lead the way."

When Fraser took one, and his finger brushed her palm, her breath caught. As his eyes rose to hers, an unexpected ripple of awareness washed over her followed by a wave of heat. When his pupils flared, she knew he felt it too. Not slow, blossoming attraction but potent explosive chemistry. A sensual connection that made her heart race and her thoughts scatter.

"I'm surprised your brother hasnae made his way back to Argyll by now." His voice was low and gravelly as his eyes stayed with hers.

"Especially considering his profession."

"Och, nay," she whispered. Her eyes remained with his a moment longer before she finally managed to tear them away and looked at the stones again. "These are cursed as is the treasure. They have brought nothing but grief to our kin, and well my brother knows it." She frowned. "There is nothing but blood and heartache in their wake, and there will be nothing but the same in their future." Her eyes returned to his. "A path I fear ye and I now walk down, Fraser."

He didn't seem all that concerned. But then she suspected fear was not something he was accustomed to. His courage ran deep.

"Then we shall walk this path together, lass." He handed her the stone. "And mayhap we will finally put your history to rest, so your future isnae so shrouded."

"Thank ye," she whispered, truly grateful as she put the stones away then urged him to get some rest.

Sleep did not come easy as she continued watching him long after he drifted off. She could almost imagine that mayhap her ancestors had sent him to her. A means of protection through the troubling times ahead. Mayhap even something more. She frowned at that thought, not sure she was ready.

After all, with love came eventual heartache and the risk of great loss.

As intended, she saw to Fraser for two more days during which they spent ample time talking and getting to know one another. As much as was possible, that is. He could not share what he didn't know. And while she sensed that frustrated him to no end, he kept it well repressed. But then, he appeared quite content listening to her and seemed taken by just about anything she said. That, she surmised, helped keep his mind off himself.

"Ye think me more interesting than I really am," she chided during one of their more lively conversations. "Being a natural healer is not the most adventurous occupation."

"Yet I have felt like I was on an adventure since the moment I awoke." As always, his easy smile and the sultry promise in his eyes made her pulse race. "An adventure with ye at its verra heart."

If she had learned nothing else about Fraser MacLomain, it was that flirting came naturally to him. Point in fact, the way he had just said the word 'heart.' As though it was his heart he spoke of, and she already possessed it.

In truth, she was beginning to suspect it was the other way around. Moreover, she was beginning to think her heart had been his since the moment she found him. Which, she figured, trying to find logic in it, would only lend credence to the pretense that they were together.

That in mind, on the third morning after his fever broke, she decided it was time to take him to her village. He was doing much better than expected and she was eager to hear what Douglas had found out.

After Fraser bathed and dressed in clothing Innis had provided days ago, he stood in front of her as she looked him over. The breeches would have to do, she supposed. The boots hid their short length, but their snug fit wasn't to be helped. Nor would the favorable looks he'd likely receive from the lasses. While his untucked tunic hid the ample bulge in front and of course, the firm globes of his arse, his admirable thighs, and calves were quite obvious.

"Are ye sure ye want to present me to your parents like this, lass?" A charming grin curled up one corner of his mouth. "They may think ye've caught yourself a rogue rather than a gentleman, aye?"

She only offered a small smile in response. They would likely think a great many things.

As she expected, he was very tall and imposing when he stood. A true threat.

"Innis brought weapons." She gestured at the small stack of blades and sheathes nearby. "Take whatever ye like."

"I like them all," he rumbled, his eyes never leaving her face. "'Tis up to ye how many I choose though."

She understood his meaning. How threatening did she really want him to appear? "I think first impressions are verra important." Her sly eyes slid from the weapons to him. "Because 'twill be that impression which is carried to our enemy's ears, aye?"

"Aye, then." He nodded and proceeded to strap nearly all of them on his person with barely a flinch from their weight. Had he not still suffered residual pain from his wounds, she suspected he would have attached every last weapon.

"Do I look the part then?" He held out his arms as if offering himself up for further inspection.

"I think 'tis a look ye've worn before," she replied honestly, noticing how at ease and knowledgeable he seemed of each weapon. How he had strapped them in such a way to keep them visible yet his movements flexible. In turn, she had the feeling he knew how to hide them just as easily to trick his adversary.

"Aye, ye look the part," she assured.

"And how shall I *act* the part?" His voice had deepened along with his purposeful words.

She arched her brows, though she knew precisely what he was getting at. "How do ye mean?"

"Well, you're claiming that I'm yours, aye?" A devilish twinkle lit his eyes. "Should I romance ye in front of them all, then?" His tone turned flirtatious and playful. "Should I steal a wee kiss or two?"

"I dinnae think that's necessary quite yet," she murmured, her cheeks warming at the very thought.

"Do ye not want to be convincing then?" He shifted closer, his eyes curious, his intent obvious. "Do ye not want your enemy to know how much I love ye?" He narrowed his eyes as though glaring at said foe. "That such love would truly test my warrior's soul if any harm came to ye and yours."

"Well, when ye phrase it like that mayhap," she said softly, ensnared by his eyes, by his ever closing proximity. "A wee chaste kiss on the cheek that is…"

"Och, that is not the sort of kiss that warns others away," he scoffed. "But another sort entirely."

She had no chance to respond before he reeled her close and showed her just what sort of kiss he had in mind.

Chapter Three

FRASER KNEW THE moment he kissed Elspeth MacLauchlin that she would be his. Aye, he would play the part of her beloved until it was no longer acting. Until she realized what he foresaw for them.

The path they were supposed to walk together was not just for this endeavor but lifelong.

When he tilted his mouth more firmly over hers and ran the tip of his tongue along the seam of her lips, she allowed the kiss to deepen. So much so that it became the sort of kiss that had them both groaning before she reluctantly pulled away. Her eyes remained closed for a moment before they met his. Dewy, soft with desire, they shimmered with the promise of a bright future indeed.

"I dinnae think we need much practice," she whispered before releasing a choppy breath.

"Nay," he murmured, running the pad of his thumb along her soft jawline. "Though 'tis no hardship, lass."

For the first time since he met her, fear flashed in her eyes. Telling, considering she might have bloodthirsty pirates after her yet simple affection seemed more of a threat. Though tempted to ask her why, he felt it better left alone. At least for now. She had obviously been hurt. Mayhap a broken heart? Nay, impossible. Who would ever be so foolish to turn away the likes of her?

He had enjoyed getting to know her better over the past few days. It was clear she had a great love for nature and all it could provide. Her knowledge of herbs and the art of healing was extensive. Her intelligence unmistakable.

Though it was obvious she had traveled very little, her imagination seemed to know no bounds. If he wasn't mistaken, there was an adventurer lurking within her. Someone who occasionally dreamt of escaping her responsibilities. Maybe even a free spirit eager to live life beyond these shores. Above all, one thing became clear during their numerous conversations.

He would never tire of her.

Now that he knew what it felt like to have her in his arms and her lips against his, he felt all that much stronger. There was no turning from this nor would he want to.

Someday this lass *would* be his wife.

"Come then, 'tis time to meet my kin," she said, cutting into his thoughts as she took his hand and pulled him after her. "This eve marks my sister's eighth winter so they will be celebrating."

As he figured, they were in a cave on the shore. A lone galley with furled sails bobbed in the harbor.

"'Tis my brother's ship, *The Sea Hellion*." Both worry and longing lit her eyes as she looked at the vessel. "Though he owes his allegiance to the *Devils of the Deep*, he does as he likes and will likely have his own fleet someday."

"Despite its name, it looks peaceable," he remarked.

"Aye, right now so it doesnae draw unwanted attention," she murmured. "But when 'tis out pirating, 'tis another beastie altogether."

"What led him to such a thing?" he couldn't help but ask, not particularly impressed. "'Tis dangerous, is it not?"

And unprincipled. Not honorable at all. But he kept those thoughts to himself.

"We were attacked years ago by a rogue band of pirates." The timbre of her whisper soft response was forlorn. "'Twas then that Shaw MacDougall and his *Devils of the Deep* came to our aid." Her eyes went to the sea. "We never did know why he helped us. Some said the rogue band was his enemy. Others said it was because I had seen to a few of his crewmate's wounds after one skirmish or another."

She sighed and shook her head as she continued. "Either way, Douglas was young, thankful and angered by how defenseless he had been. So he decided to change that by swearing his allegiance right then and there." She picked up random colorful shells as they walked. "As time went on, he eventually got his own ship and began a crew that could better protect and provide for his village." Her eyes met his. "It may not be the most honorable of things, but he has done verra well by us, and 'tis a rare sort that would dare attack us now."

Fraser offered naught but a nod. While he could well understand the impetuous actions of a young lad, pirating did not strike him as the best way to have handled it. Nonetheless, he would not say as much to Elspeth. Nor would he complain just yet about her seeing to the likes of Shaw's men. No doubt they were lecherous swine's, and she was lucky they didn't rape her when given the chance.

Rather he focused on their surroundings. Where she called home. The bay was sweeping and well-sheltered, its cliffs blanketed with verdant long-stemmed grasses and vibrant wildflowers. As they climbed a gentle slope, their sweet scent mixed with the tang of the ocean.

Yet even with the splendor around them, he could only see Elspeth.

Her wild beauty complimented her surroundings. Though she might be beholden to protecting her people, there was an unbound sense about her. A sort of oneness with Scotland and the frothing sea that was hard to put into words.

Later that day, he realized it wasn't just her surroundings that seemed so much a part of her but the very community she called her own. A small village of thatched cottages tucked away between rolling hills. Their main lodge was little larger than the rest, but it seemed a warm and welcoming retreat for a flourishing community.

Though at first, it appeared there was no leader of any sort, it soon became apparent Elspeth and Douglas provided that stability. So it was no wonder her brother had urged her to return. Not only was she the town healer, but by all accounts a voice of reason. Someone very much liked. So said the bountiful smiles she received everywhere she went.

Her parents and two younger siblings were as he imagined they would be. As kind-hearted as Elspeth. And, based on her father's sharp assessment of Fraser, just as intelligent.

"So ye met by the sea, did ye?" her da said, his eyes going from Fraser to Elspeth. "And you're in love with the lad already, aye?" Dubious, he shook his head. "Is that not a wee bit fast, lassie?"

Elspeth had decided against the truth if for no other reason than that Fraser had healed so quickly. These were superstitious times, after all. Not to mention, he had most likely been battling on or near the sea. Not something a village that remained wary of seafaring strangers needed to know.

"Och, Husband." Her ma smiled kindly at Fraser before looking at her father. "As ye well know, love doesnae have a time limit." Mischievousness lit her eyes. "Ours certainly didnae."

"Aye," he conceded, easily swayed by his wife's amorous look because he soon clasped hands with Fraser and welcomed him.

Innis had stayed on the ship to keep an eye on things, but Douglas joined them, evidently reporting nothing of consequence to Elspeth. Or so he assumed based on the brief time they spoke with one another.

It was obvious that her younger sisters Arabel and Greer were the apples of Elspeth's eye as she gave them the shells she had collected. Soon after, she left Fraser in Douglas' capable hands so she could spend some time alone with them.

"I dinnae know what she would do without them," Douglas said softly as he handed him a mug of ale. "Or them her."

"'Tis good to be so close with kin," Fraser replied, not sure why he said it when he had nothing to substantiate it. Only that he knew it without question.

"Aye," Douglas agreed, as they walked through the village. "Ye are verra convincing in this part ye play with my sister." His knowing but wary eyes slid Fraser's way. "Too convincing I'd say."

"Would ye then?" Fraser took a swig and shrugged. "She's a bonny lass. 'Tis not a hard part to play."

"Yet the way ye look at her when she's not looking at ye is telling indeed," he murmured. "So ye'll want to be careful, friend."

The way he said 'friend' told Fraser he was anything but.

So was this a brotherly warning or something more? "And why is that?"

"Because though she is strong, her heart is still fragile…bruised…"

"So it has been broken," Fraser supplied when Douglas trailed off. Honestly, he was surprised her brother had said as much to begin with.

"Aye, it has been broken," he whispered. "Well and truly."

He realized that Douglas' revelation was more than a mere warning. More than a brother looking out for his sister. Nothing was as simple as it appeared.

But then Elspeth was not a simple lass by any means.

That became abundantly clear as day turned into evening. She seemed to play a part in everyone's life from the baker to the blacksmith. Each and every one radiated pleasure when she spent time with them. From the youngest to the oldest, she was for all intents and purposes a guiding light.

"Will ye dance with me then, kind sir?" came a small voice. The merry crowd was dancing around a fire strategically placed so that it could not be spied from the sea.

When he glanced down, it was into wee Greer's wide eyes. He offered his most charming smile. "Would any lad dare say nay?"

"They would be foolish if they did." Impatient, she clasped her hands behind her back as she leaned from foot to foot in anticipation and notched her chin in challenge. "And ye dinnae strike me as the foolish sort."

He cocked a brow. "Nay?"

"Och, nay." She shook her head, her blond curls bobbing. "Not if ye love Elspeth." Her hazel eyes narrowed. "Do ye then, kind sir?"

"Love Elspeth?" His eyes went to her as she danced and laughed, her auburn highlights afire as she swirled. "Aye, lassie, I think mayhap I do."

Greer frowned. "*Mayhap*?"

"Nay, not 'mayhap' but most assuredly," he exclaimed, meaning it. "I love your sister, lassie."

"Aye, then." She considered him, still rocking back and forth with pent-up energy. "Will ye promise to protect her no matter what? Her and Douglas always protect us so 'twould be good that she has her own valiant knight to defend her."

"I will protect her," he assured. With his life.

"Promise me, then," she persisted, her steady eyes on his despite her fidgeting. "'Twill be your gift to me on my eighth winter."

Touched by her heartfelt request, he took immediate action and behaved as the knight she sought him to be. With a flourish done in such a way that firelight sparkled off his blade, he withdrew his weapon, sunk to one knee, then lowered his head over his horizontal sword.

"I vow on this sword and on my good honor that I will protect and defend your sister Elspeth till my last dying breath."

The crowd quieted, taken by the spectacle, as little Greer stared down her nose at him and considered his offer. That didn't last long, however. Clearly taken by his gallant gesture, she nodded her head and grinned. "I accept your offer, kind knight." She lifted her hand. "Ye may stand now."

"Aye, then." He met her grin as he stood, sheathed his blade, bent at the waist and offered her his hand with another dashing flourish. "Might I have this dance, lassie?"

Soon enough, he learned one more thing about himself. He quite enjoyed dancing. Not just with Greer but with wee Arabel then her ma and eventually Elspeth herself. Sure to remain the wooing lad, he danced a merry jig to the pipes with her, enchanted by her laughter before he finally pulled her close.

Her cheeks were flushed and her eyes bright as she rested a hand on his chest. At first, he thought she meant to put distance between them, but that wasn't the case at all. Instead, she fiddled absently with the edge of his tunic as their eyes held.

"Ye are well liked," she said softly. "By all of us."

"'Tis good," he murmured, overly aware of her petite body against his, of the warmth of her back through her clothing. "Ye look verra bonny this eve, lass."

"Thank ye," she whispered.

The truth was she looked far more than just 'verra bonny.' She wore a deep green dress not tied up but flowing around her ankles. Though her cleavage was hidden, the dress was revealing enough that her curves were unmistakable. Her hair hung in silky waves, haloing fair skin and magnificent eyes only amplified by firelight.

"'Tis shocking ye arenae already taken," he said softly as he kept one arm around her waist and cupped the back of her smooth neck with his free hand. While some might think he was trying to get to the root of what Douglas had implied earlier, he wasn't. Not really. He genuinely meant it.

When a mixture of pleasure and distress flashed in her eyes, he whispered close to her ear, "Tell me your thoughts, lass. Tell me what troubles ye."

While initially, he thought she would pull away based on how she tensed, she did not. Instead, her eyes met his, and she swallowed hard.

"Shh," he whispered, gently caressing her neck, trying to ease the tension knotting her delicate muscles. He would know of this man that broke her heart. Who had caused her such pain. "Surely, 'tis not that bad."

"'Tis though," she whispered, her eyes suddenly haunted and sad. "'Tis verra bad when ye lose both your husband and bairn at the same time."

Chapter Four

ABOUT THE LAST thing she had intended to do was tell Fraser about her lost kin, but something about him drew it out of her. She *wanted* him to know. After all these years, she *wanted* to let someone in.

"I'm so verra sorry, lass," he whispered, his gaze compassionate.

She swallowed back emotion and nodded. "'Twas many years ago during that first raid I spoke of." Her eyes drifted to her brother. "'Tis why Douglas followed the path he did...why I supported him." She looked at Fraser again. "And why I remain grateful to Shaw MacDougall. If not for him, we might have lost everyone that day."

"Aye," he murmured, yet she saw the conflict in his eyes. He was no fan of piracy. Even so, he kept it to himself as he urged her to rest her cheek against his chest.

"My husband was killed," she whispered, still seeing it as though it had happened yesterday. "But not my daughter, Aileann...not that day anyway."

Fraser remained respectfully silent, stroking her hair in comfort as she continued. Her daughter's sparkling eyes and auburn curls arose in her mind's eye. "She was barely four winters old…a baby really…"

Flashes of that evening haunted her. Aileann's cries for Elspeth as she was snatched up then swept away into the dark void of night. Her mournful little wails as she was callously ripped away from the only life she knew.

"They tried to save her. Douglas, Innis, even Shaw." She shook her head. "But whoever took her slipped away leaving no trace." Refusing to give into tears, she blinked away moisture as her eyes rose to Fraser's. "Shaw might seem like a ruthless bastard, but he has a soft spot when it comes to innocent wee ones."

She released a ragged breath before she went on. "I've continued seeing to the wounds of Shaw's men on and off over the years, and he's kept me apprised of any news of her whereabouts…or lack thereof."

Though she remained hopeful for far longer than she should have, she had left that sentiment behind years ago. It just hurt too much to be anything but logical, even indifferent on the rare occasion she could manage it. Best to see things for what they really were. A pirate took her little girl, and nothing good could ever come of that. She would have been sold into slavery of one sort or another. Nothing but relentless horror would have awaited her.

Elspeth pressed her lips together and fought another wave of emotion as she rested her cheek against Fraser's chest again. There was only one thing they would have used her darling daughter for, and she refused to think on it.

Instead, afloat in the safe harbor of his arms, she indulged in the rare fantasy of a happy ending for her child. Because if by the grace of God, she had survived, she would be nigh on twelve winters old now.

And if she had made it that far, perhaps not all was lost.

Nothing was said for a while after that, and she was grateful for it. That day was hard to think about let alone share. So she closed her eyes, inhaled deeply, immersed herself in his spicy scent and did what she always did. Let the memories drift away. Eventually, they would come back. They always did. But for now, there was just him. And the way he felt against her.

The kiss they had shared earlier.

A kiss that had very much swept her off her feet.

She had known at that moment he was the one for her. There would be no other who made her feel the way he did. It was quick. Too quick, some might say. But it was real and far different than what she had experienced before. With her husband, they'd been very young, and it had been more of a childhood friendship turned to mild infatuation. With Fraser, it was immediate and far from mild.

He was her destiny.

She knew it without question.

So it was no surprise that as the weeks passed, their feelings only grew. Though the entirety of his memory did not return, bits and pieces continued to surface. A fact readily seen as he and Innis fought one another on the rocky shore as she gathered oysters.

His battle skills were astounding.

He had been well trained.

As it happened, rumors of treasure in connection with her kin all but vanished, and things had returned to normal. Though Fraser seemed intent to remain by her side despite the waning threat, she sensed a restlessness growing inside him. A longing in his eyes when he gazed in the direction of Argyll.

He was curious about his clan, and she didn't blame him. If it were her, she would want to return to her people too. She would be eager to get answers about herself. To understand who she was and why she ended up broken on the shores of the North Sea.

"Bloody hell!" Innis sputtered as Fraser drove him back so quickly that he fell flat on his arse. Half a blink later, Fraser's blade was against his neck as he roared, "Yield!"

His face flaming red to match his hair, Innis' bright green eyes narrowed in challenge before he started to chuckle.

Rather than allow his blade to cut Innis' neck due to untimely levity, Fraser pulled it away. Chuckling as well, he shook his head and held out his hand. "Ye mad bastard."

Innis continued laughing as he allowed Fraser to pull him up. Comrades from the start, they patted each other on the shoulder in goodwill. Though she knew Innis had always desired her and might see Fraser as competition, they got along well regardless. But then they seemed of a similar nature which as far as she could tell had a great deal to do with battling.

Her apprentice Audric sat nearby bundling herbs as he quietly watched. Every once in a while, she sensed he longed to pick up a blade, but it went against his healing nature. Perhaps in time, he might change his mind. Because even healers needed to know how to defend themselves. And sometimes, however difficult it may be, inflicting a wound helped to better understand how it might heal.

"Have ye had much luck finding oysters, lass?" Innis asked as they joined her. "'Tis a good storm out yonder churning the sea bed aplenty."

"Aye," she agreed, eying the dark skies in the distance before her gaze returned to the shore. "'Tis also the same storm creating these waves and Lord knows they dinnae make oyster collecting all that easy."

The corner of Innis' eyes crinkled as he grinned and eyed the water. "Nay, I dinnae suppose they do."

Meanwhile, Fraser had been meandering around and scooped up several oysters enviously fast. All of which he dropped in her pouch before he offered her the mischievous crooked grin she so enjoyed.

"Thank ye," she murmured.

"'Twas my pleasure, lass." He dropped a kiss on her cheek, then shifted his lips closer to hers, teasing, before he pulled away.

"The plaid looks good," she remarked, eying him with appreciation.

She had worked tirelessly to mend his ripped and tattered MacLomain tartan. Now he wore nothing but the plaid wrapped around his waist and over his shoulder. Another means to test her, she was sure. Because there was no finer sight than Fraser dressed as he was with his chiseled muscles bared to the world.

"I think he enjoys his vanity fed," Innis muttered as he grinned and rolled his eyes at the hill behind them. A hill that had hosted many a lass over the past few hours. Lasses, quite assuredly, out for a late-afternoon stroll to enjoy the view. And though they would claim otherwise, that view had nothing to do with the lovely bay.

Even Audric was aware of the women, his cheeks turning red when he dared a random peek over his shoulder.

"Well, I would see Fraser's vanity challenged," Elspeth murmured, not speaking of his good looks as she picked up one of several swords Innis had brought down. One suited to her size. She met Fraser's eyes in challenge. "Do ye accept, then?"

His brows perked in interest. "Ye know how to fight?"

"Of course," she replied, wide-eyed. "'Twould be foolish in these tryin' times not to, aye?"

"I suppose 'twould," he concurred, a new spark in his eyes. One, she realized, born of a man who appreciated a woman who knew how to defend herself.

"So will ye then?" She made a show of testing the weight of the blade and even executed a few novice swings to prove she was good but not *that* good.

When a small smirk hovered on his lips, and his eyes narrowed on her grip, she knew he had her figured out.

"'Tis a good enough method making your opponent think ye cocky rather than talented," he acknowledged. "But you'll want to work some on your expression."

"My expression?"

"Aye, 'tis that of one with confidence, not insecurity." He stepped close and brushed the pad of his weapon-roughened thumb between her brows. "It should furrow here as though ye are concentrating verra hard indeed." Then he grazed it along her lips. "These should be turned down and mayhap wobble a wee bit as ye begin to doubt yourself. As if ye just realized ye took on more than ye can handle facing off with your particular enemy."

After that, he dusted the outer edge of her brow indicating her eyes. "And these, of course, are your best weapon if you're fighting a lad. Use them to look him over as if sizing him up." A knowing gleam lit his eyes. "A look as if you're trying to determine his weaknesses but realize mayhap there's something to be attracted to instead."

"I willnae do that," she rebuffed, chuckling despite herself. "'Tis foolish."

"I dinnae know." Innis stroked the braids in his beard as he contemplated Elspeth. "I think Fraser is right. Especially when it comes to ye."

"'Twill make me seem daft!" she retaliated.

"'Twill make ye seem as your rival likely expects ye to be," Fraser counseled, still close enough that she could feel his heat. "A lass with a proper eye to pleasing a lad instead of a disobedient hellion trying to be something she's not."

When she narrowed her eyes, he merely shrugged and grinned. "I didnae say I agree with that mindset." He stepped back and held his sword at arm's length. "I'm more the sort that enjoys a wee lassie with a bit of backbone."

"Good then." She straightened said backbone and held her blade at the ready, wishing she wore trousers instead of a skirt.

They eyed one another and circled before she came at him fast. When he dodged, she spun quickly, came in low only for him to leap back with a grin of approval.

"Ye use your size to your advantage," he praised. "And keep your movements quick but small."

"Aye." She ducked beneath the swing of his blade. "Douglas always said to conserve my energy. Especially when fighting a seasoned warrior."

Innis guffawed. "Well, you're certainly fighting such now, lassie!"

"Your brother's words were wise," Fraser conceded as they continued battling. While she knew he was holding back some, she could tell by his random nods of approval that it wasn't as much as he thought it would be.

Yet as they continued crossing swords, she saw something shift in his eyes moments before he came at her a little harder. While she initially thought he was competitive and could not help himself, she soon realized it was for another reason altogether.

He truly cared about her well-being and wanted her to fight the best she could.

So as they fought and her energy waned, he offered not only praise where it was due but pointed out her every weakness. An elbow held too high on a swing. The incorrect angle of her knee when lunging. Breathing too heavily when she should be trying to measure her breaths for certain movements and speed. His was a well-balanced dance. A very specific manipulation of the body that included a mixture of thought out planning and spontaneity.

By the time they were finished, she was sore in places she had never felt pain.

"Thank ye," she managed, as she tossed aside her blade, planted her hands on her knees and tried to catch her breath. "I will be feeling this for days, I imagine."

"'Tis good." He smiled. "'Twill give ye a better idea of what needs strengthening."

Though not a lewd look by any means, as their eyes held, she got the strongest impression he longed to test other muscles as well. To see how limber she really was.

While they greatly desired one another and he had stolen many a kiss over the past few weeks, they had not yet laid together. Even though she longed for the moment, something held her back. Fear, she supposed. Not only of giving herself over entirely to a man after all these years but then possibly losing him. Aye, Fraser was stronger than most, but even the mightiest could fall beneath a well-aimed blade.

Yet deep down she knew at this point fear was a lost cause. There was no need to lie with him to know she would never be the same if she lost him. He had made his way into her heart and losing him was unthinkable. Which brought her mind back to his clan and the inevitable loss looming on the horizon when he finally sought them out.

"Was Douglas not hoping to return before the storm?" Fraser asked, drawing her eyes back to the sea. Blackening clouds lay thick in the distance, peppering the blues and greens of the churning ocean in heavy shadows.

"Aye, he said as much," Innis replied as they gathered their weapons and Elspeth snatched up her bag of oysters. "But 'tis more likely he'll wait it out now."

While she always worried about her brother, he was an excellent seaman, so she set aside concern as they returned to the village for a bit. A good catch had been brought in, and there was plenty of sea trout and even some salmon to be enjoyed.

Fraser seemed in a particularly amorous mood, so she wasn't all that surprised when he suggested they eat dinner in their cave. That was what they had come to call it. *Their* cave. Mostly because they enjoyed spending time alone there. Their conversations were long and varied, and laughter was not uncommon. He had a sense of humor that kept her mood light.

"There was a reason I wanted to come here this eve, lass," he murmured as they sat together sometime later sharing a dram of whisky. A fire crackled as rain poured, and thunder rumbled. He brushed a lock of hair out of her eyes as his words softened even more. "Something I wished to speak with ye about."

"Aye, then," she whispered, barely able to get the words out. Was this it? Was he finally going to tell her that it was time for him to leave?

"'Tis about us." His hand slipped into hers. "About how much I've come to care for ye…love ye."

"Aye, then," she repeated, not capable of much else. He loved her yet he was leaving? Why bother telling her just to break her heart? Did he have no compassion?

"I want to be with ye." His eyes never wavered. "Do ye ken, lass?"

She nodded dumbly. Then do not leave, she wanted to say. Do not go, she wanted to rail.

"Good," he whispered as he slid something onto her finger. Her eyes dropped to the stunning ring made of bits of pearl and sparkling coral before they whipped back to his.

"'Tis not much," he began before he cupped her cheek and finally said what he had been leading up to.

"Will ye become my wife, Elspeth MacLauchlin?" he said. "Will ye marry me?"

Chapter Five

FRASER HAD NO idea if it was too soon to ask Elspeth to marry him but he could not wait a moment longer. He had been eager to make her his since their first kiss. Eager to make her his if only she would have him.

Her moist eyes dropped to the ring before returning to him. "Ye want to marry me, then?"

"Aye." He wrapped his fingers with hers. "I think mayhap I've wanted to since I first laid eyes on ye."

"This is not what I expected," she whispered as she looked at the ring again. "'Tis verra beautiful. Excellent craftsmanship." She peered at it more closely. "Rare treasure indeed." Her eyes returned to his. "Ye made this yourself, then?"

"I did."

Though minor, he took creating the ring as discovering another missing piece of who he had been and shared as much. Instead of focusing on the fact she had yet to answer his question, he colored his proposal with the making of the jewelry.

"With thoughts only of ye, I searched the ocean floor day after day for the perfect pieces to sand down and string together." He touched one of the pieces of coral. "Pink to match the stain of your bonny cheeks when ye look at me." He touched another. "Ivory to match your soft skin when the morning light caresses it." Then a pearl. "These to match the sparkle of your eyes." Then one more bit. "And, of course, the silvery coral in betwixt."

"What does that remind ye of?" she whispered.

"In truth, I havenae quite figured it out yet." He tried not to look guilty as he offered a lopsided grin. "I but thought it complimentary to the others." He shrugged. "And keeping true to rumors of my clan, a wee bit mystical in appearance, aye?"

Her blossoming smile stilled at those last words. "Aye, verra mystical."

"What is it, lass?" he said softly, tilting her chin until her eyes stayed with his. "Do ye not welcome my proposal then?"

"Nay, I do." Her heart was in her eyes. "But I dinnae ken it…"

"How so?"

"Do ye not long to find your clan, Fraser?" she asked. "To discover what happened to ye?" Her brows flew together in concern. "For all ye know ye could verra well be married to another."

"Nay." He shook his head, having already mulled it over. "I am not. I feel that verra strongly." His eyes never deviated from hers. "As to seeking out my clan, aye, I will eventually." He squeezed her hand in reassurance. "But I will return to ye, Elspeth. I know your place is with your people."

"As yours could verra well be with yours," she countered. "Ye could be their chieftain." She shook her head. "'Twould not surprise me of a man like ye."

"Aye, mayhap," he replied. "But if I'm of a clan the likes of the MacLomains, do ye not think they have a replacement?"

"Until your safe return," she argued.

"Lass." He cupped her cheeks and searched her eyes. "Aye, 'tis true there are plenty of possibilities when it comes to what I yet know about myself but one thing is verra clear and part of who I am." His words met his passion. "And that is *ye*. How I feel when I'm with ye and what I want from my future no matter what." He brushed his lips across hers then whispered, "Ye and no one else."

Her eyes moistened even more as they stayed with his and while she offered no answer, she *did* kiss him. Once, twice, then a third time before those kisses deepened. Though she wasn't giving her response in words, he very much felt she was in actions as she lay back and pulled him down after her.

The moment had come at long last.

A moment he had imagined day and night.

More than ready to have her, he kissed his way down her soft, slender neck as he deftly worked at the ties on her dress. Her chest rose and fell rapidly as he dropped kisses along her delicate collarbone, before returning to her lips.

He fully intended to take his time and enjoy every last part of her. Learn where she liked being touched most and how she liked to be touched there. As their tongues tangled, he lowered her top just enough to expose more cleavage. And just enough to keep her hovering on the edge of need, as he slowly built her desire.

As he worked his way back down and dropped kisses along her breasts, her breathing grew choppier. It became more ragged still as inch by inch he ran his hand up her small calf, over her dainty knee then bit by agonizing bit, up her slender thigh beneath her skirts.

He blew lightly on her sensitive skin, enjoying the gooseflesh that fanned out. Gentle yet eager, he cupped her breast over her clothing and returned to her lips. When she began releasing small moans as he deepened the kiss, he continued exploring her thigh until he reached her center. Her lips broke from his as she arched and released a throaty groan.

He could listen to that forever.

The sweet, unabashed sound of her pleasure.

Determined to do just that, he manipulated the soft flesh between her thighs while he made his way back to her tempting breasts. Rather than lower her top all the way just yet, he pulled a taut nipple into his mouth despite the material.

Mesmerized, he never took his eyes off her face as her arousal grew. Her lips were slightly apart in bliss, and her eyes shut as he brought her closer and closer to release. Soon her groans turned to cries. Small wails of pleasure that mixed with cracks of thunder and roaring waves.

Yet through it all, he heard something that didn't belong.

Something not right.

When he stilled, and whispered, "Quiet lass," her eyes shot to his in alarm.

In between cracks of thunder he heard it again.

A terrified cry on the wind.

Where was that coming from? What was happening? Then he realized.

They were under attack.

"Bloody hell." He leapt to his feet and yanked his boots on. "'Tis the village."

Fear in her eyes, Elspeth made the sign of the cross over her chest, and half sobbed, half muttered under her breath, "Please, God, not again."

She adjusted her dress and pulled her boots on as well.

When their eyes met, he shook his head. "You'll stay here where 'tis safe, lass."

"I most certainly willnae!" She shook her head, a stubborn notch to her chin as she pointed at the exit. "That's *my* kin out there. *My* people!"

While he could force her to stay, he knew full well she would never forgive him. He also had the strongest feeling that if anybody tried to do that to him when it came to his kin, he'd likely kill them.

"Fine then," he muttered as he strapped on his weapons and gave her a few daggers. The only sword they had was too big for her.

"Stay close to me," he ordered as they left the cave. "And stay to the shadows until I've had a chance to assess the situation."

When she didn't respond, he stopped short and glowered at her. She meant far too much for him to accept anything but firm compliance. "Do ye ken, lass?"

"Aye," she muttered, nudging him. "Let's go then!"

Though her response wasn't nearly as assuring as he would have liked, they had no time. The villagers' cries were only growing more intense.

Cold rain fell in heavy sheets, blinding them to the bay. If a ship or even a fleet were out there, they would never know. So there was no way to know who they were dealing with.

An enemy from land or sea.

Yet as they made their way up the slick, muddy hillside, his dread only grew as he gave it more thought. While not overly familiar with the way of seafaring criminals and their shady scheming, he began to see a savvy plan at work.

What if the Spanish had tested the village with that rumor of Elspeth's kins' treasure? Not necessarily to seek out whether or not the rumor was true, but to see how the village would react to a potential pirate invasion. How would they fortify themselves? How often would Douglas remain in port?

Naturally, this would all be in preparation for a strike.

And though it seemed nautically unwise, would such a storm not create the perfect cover to attack? Especially considering Douglas was not here? And while yes, Elspeth had fabricated her own rumor about

Fraser, he was but one man. That, to his mind, would not sway pirates. Not when it came to treasure and mayhap even a long-standing vendetta against the MacLauchlin's.

"Oh dear Lord," Elspeth cried when they reached the outskirts of the village and crouched behind a rock. "They're everywhere!" She spoke through clenched teeth. "Not Spanish but *French*."

They truly were everywhere and pirates, all.

Ruthless, they attacked without mercy, and several villagers had already fallen. The only real hope they seemed to have was Innis. He fought like a madman, roaring all the while. Even through the driving rain, there was no missing the fury in his eyes or the black intent in his heart as he cut down several Frenchmen in a row.

When Elspeth surged forward, Fraser pulled her back down beside him and put a hand over her mouth. The last thing they needed was to give away their position. While he understood her anguish and did not blame her impetuousness, she needed to remain calm, and he told her as much.

"Stay here," he whispered, meeting her eyes in the darkness. "I will go fight, and I will protect your kin." He shook his head. "If ye leave this spot and they attack ye, all might be lost because I will defend ye before anyone else." He narrowed his eyes. "Would ye have that on your conscience then? That ye didnae listen, and your kin suffered for it?"

"Nay," she sputtered as he slowly removed his hand. Tears mixed with rain in her horrified eyes. "I will stay, Fraser. Just go. Please. *Now*." She pushed him yet clenched his tunic at the same time as if subconsciously undecided whether she wanted him to go. "But be careful, aye?"

"Aye." His request was never more urgent, his reminder never more heartfelt. "And ye *stay here*."

He couldn't lose her. He refused to. Yet he could no longer remain by her side. He must save these people. Defend them. So he had to put faith in her good sense. Their eyes held for another brief moment. Long enough that she saw the gravity of his concern and understood the amount of trust he put in her.

Then he raced into the mayhem.

This was unimaginable. Shameful. Men were being slaughtered, and their wives dragged into cottages, at the whim of the demons who had them. Even children were not spared from the savagery. The pure horror. When he saw a pirate backhand wee Greer, his inner berserker took over.

A side of him he wasn't wholly sure existed until this moment.

A side that somewhere in the back of his mind he wished Greer did not have to see.

Yet he would not be stopped. Not until every last pirate fell beneath his blade. Roaring with rage, he whipped a dagger into the man's forehead before he yanked him away from Greer and sliced his throat open for good measure.

Then he focused on the next and the next, unleashing pure hell on every pirate in his path. He drove his sword into one man's gut as he side-kicked another. While he pulled his sword free, he punched anyone who dared to come at him.

When two more were brave enough to try him, he whipped a dagger into one man's windpipe then started to parry with the other. All the while, he kicked and punched anybody that approached him before swiftly ending the pirate he fought.

After that, it all became a blur as he reveled in the glory of battle. In the unequaled adrenaline rush of destroying his enemy, and staining the ground with their blood. He anticipated and used everything the storm provided from the slick mud underfoot to the jarring cracks of thunder. Even the blinding flashes of lightning could be used in the right context.

When he ran out of weapons, he grabbed more off the dead.

Not only did he lay waste to those who came at him but found time to slip into cottages and end any who dared harm a lass. At one point in the midst of battle, his eyes met Innis,' and they nodded. There was no disputing that he and his fellowman fought well alongside one another.

Only when the last man standing fell beneath his blade and the roar on his lips died did he finally hear Greer's screams.

"Ye promised to protect her!" she wailed, sobbing hysterically. "Ye promised to protect her, but she's *gone*!"

He blinked several times, still caught in a haze of battlelust before what she meant struck him like a punch to the gut.

Elspeth had been taken.

"Guard the villagers," he roared to Innis as he raced down the hillside, slipping, sliding and even leaping half the time. He wiped his hand across his eyes, trying to see through the rain and darkness but it was impossible.

"Elspeth," he roared over and over.

Yet there was nothing.

No response.

This could not be happening. They could not have taken her.

As he raced for the shore, he tossed aside his weapons, yanked off his boots, and ran into the icy water. He ignored the sting of the rocks underfoot as he kept scanning the horizon, waiting for a lightning flash. Anything to help him see through the darkness.

He kept roaring her name, fighting the waves, when he sensed something behind him. When he spun, it was to see a bloodied pirate staggering into the ocean.

Enraged, Fraser stayed low and headed his way until he caught the man unaware, drove him back and slammed him down on the ground. Shaking with fury, he wedged the one dagger left on him against the enemy's neck and ground out, "Where is she?"

He recognized the man. He had slain several villagers and nearly raped a young lass.

Under the assumption his time had come to an end, the enemy only chuckled, his rancid breath foul. "Ye'll not see her again, mate. She belongs to the cap'n now till he tires of her and gives her to the rest of 'em." He bared his rotten teeth in glee. "Then they'll toss 'er overboard when they're through with her." His chuckle sounded insane as he thrust his hips lewdly to get his point across. "Right where the over used rung out wench will belong."

A strange inner calm swept over Fraser as he kept the blade tight against his enemy's throat and turned an eye to the sea. As he did thunder rocked the heavens, and bright lightning splintered across the sky. That's when his worst fear was confirmed.

Two pirate ships were sailing away in the distance.

As if mocking Fraser himself, their black flags flew in dark, sinister triumph. They had her. They had his love, and things were never going to be the same. Not so long as she was anywhere but in his arms.

It seemed everything good in the world vanished at that moment.

Simply snuffed out.

What those pirates didn't know was that they had awakened a beast that night. One that would do everything in his power to get back what they had taken from him. When lightning flashed again, he memorized their flags. When it flashed once more, he noted every last detail of one ship. When it flashed again, he forged the other ship in his memory.

All the while as the ocean swirled around them on the rocky shore, he kept a death grip on the man beneath him. At long last, when good and ready, he turned dead eyes his way. As it would be told for years to come by the very man he held down, it was as if he stared into the devil's own eyes that night.

As if he witnessed the fiery pits of Hell.

But then Hell had only truly just begun as Fraser leaned down close and made a promise he kept.

"Ye'll not suffer death this night," he growled through clenched teeth. "Instead, your every waking moment will be a living nightmare until you've led me to your captain." His eyes narrowed. "Until I have my lass back." With nothing but vengeance in his heart, he offered a wicked grin. "Your wretched, cursed life just took a dark turn, slave. Welcome to my crew, *The Sea Hellions*."

Chapter Six

Cruden Bay, Scotland
Two Years Later

SITTING QUIETLY BY a dying fire with an empty dram of whisky dangling from limp fingers, Fraser watched his fellow pirates with a detached eye. Wenches meandered about, more around than usual with so many ships in port. When one sat on his lap and wiggled her arse against his cock, he absently repositioned her on his knee.

"So yer not wantin' a wee taste tonight then, aye Cap'n MacLomain?" she slurred.

"Nay," he murmured, slurring a bit himself as he kept a keen eye on one ship in particular. "I'm wantin' a bit of something else though."

"Aye then," she muttered, disappointment in her eyes as she took his meaning and flounced off.

The truth of it was, he wasn't drunk but found it the best way to behave around here. After all, a pirate that didn't take advantage of whisky and women when in port was suspicious indeed. Because the devil knew that *might* just mean they were clever and up to no good.

"Ye see it then?" Innis murmured as he plunked down beside him and took a hearty swig from his mug.

"Aye," he responded, paying particular attention to the crew as the Scottish brigantine in question dropped anchor. "And soon enough I'll not only see but hear what she has to say."

Innis nodded, well aware that Fraser had taken full advantage of his good looks, mock charm and of course, coin to employ several wenches here. All of which gladly did his bidding.

"Ye do have a way with the lassies," Innis muttered around a grin as he shook his head. "I'm not sure if 'tis your good or foul nature that attracts them."

He had long developed a method of acting the sea-hardened black-guard around them when in company but treated them completely different when alone. Rather than lay with them half the time, he offered a kind word or two. Theirs was not an easy profession, and he had seen it destroy many. With him, they knew they were safe and more often than not made good coin without having to spread their legs.

"We'll avenge her death," Innis vowed softly. "We'll avenge our Elspeth."

Very little got past his hardened heart nowadays except talk of that.

Her.

Always her.

How bonny she had been. The love they had shared. He could almost see her again, standing on the shores of her village. How her eyes and hair sparkled in the sun as she grinned and dared him to battle her. It sometimes seemed when he gazed inland from the sea that she still stood there, tempting him with her wild spirit. Waving to him that he might come home.

Then, as it always did when he thought of her, darkness shadowed his mind at the horrible fate she had suffered. A cruel death at the hands of his mortal enemy, Estienne Du Blanc and his crew of despicable renegades.

As Fate would have it, the day she was initially taken had marked the beginning of Fraser's legacy. People far and wide spoke of the destruction that had befallen pirates when they dared to attack a small village in Stonehaven Bay. With wide eyes, they whispered in hushed awe-struck tones of a cutthroat but righteous warrior pirate that was the Robin Hood of the seas.

Yet, as he had ensured over the past two years, his fellow pirates saw him as anything but. He had become Fraser "The Rogue" MacLomain with good reason. Whether or not he truly was, he painted himself as an unprincipled, devious, swindling bastard with a cold heart and a vicious sword hand. On occasion, especially of late, he was beginning to think he might just be all of those things.

Though tempted to take the MacAlpin name like so many Britannia pirate kings before him, he stuck with MacLomain. He wanted his enemy to know *exactly* who was coming for him. He wanted him to quake in fear at the mere mention of his name.

With that firmly in mind, he had long since 'gone on account' and embraced piratehood with avid gusto. Though infuriated by Elspeth's kidnapping, Douglas proved thankful that at least Fraser had been there to help Innis save their people.

Like Fraser, Douglas embraced his rage and gladly took him on as part of his crew. Since then, they had amassed two more ships of which Fraser and Innis became their own captains. All flew *The Sea Hellions* flag, though their allegiance remained solely to Shaw "Savage" Mac-Dougall. Because had she still been here, Elspeth would not have had it any other way.

Even so, since the three of them began pirating together, their sole purpose was to find Elspeth and reap vengeance. Sadly, however, they were too late. She was slain over a year and a half ago. Used by Estienne's men until, as rumor had it, there was nothing left of her, and she was tossed overboard. It was said Estienne even went so far as to curse her spirit to forever walk aimlessly in the watery grave of Davy Jones' Locker.

Her death did not lessen *The Sea Hellions'* pursuit, but intensified it, fanning the flames of their ever-growing hatred. So now, with blasphemous fury in their hearts, they remained dead set on revenge.

Unfortunately, much to Fraser's chagrin, the enemy had managed to stay one step ahead of them. Mainly because Estienne knew that *The Sea Hellions* were after his head. That made him especially vigilant in his evasion. A coward who enjoyed the benefit of favorable connections. Namely, a rival pirate crew of the *Devils of the Deep*.

Yet now it seemed that rival crew was going to work in their favor.

"Your dog," Douglas muttered, tearing him from his thoughts as he knocked Roddy to his knees in front of Fraser and tossed him the end of his leash.

Fraser nodded and tossed Douglas a skin of his favorite whisky in return.

Knowing full well where to go, Roddy, his captive from Elspeth's village scrambled to Fraser's side, sat obediently, then lowered his head. His sole job was to discreetly eye the comings and goings of others and report back to his master. Well tamed beneath Fraser's rage, he had come in handy on many occasions.

"They're not in port long," Douglas said softly as his steady eyes stayed on Fraser. Elspeth's brother might seem nonplussed, but he knew anticipation lurked behind his shadowed gaze. "Mayhap an hour at most."

"'Tis long enough to wet their cocks," Fraser murmured, his eyes on the wench he had just sent to do his bidding.

Though Douglas had started out in charge of the three of them, as time went on, they began looking more to Fraser. Elspeth's brother didn't seem to mind as Fraser not only excelled at manipulation and cunning, but had an uncanny talent for sniffing out treasure. Leadership came naturally and seafaring almost second nature. In truth, he found the ocean soothing whether on smooth waters or in a raging storm.

Not to mention he felt closer to Elspeth when at sea.

As if by some impossible feat, the endless water might someday return her to him.

Douglas eyed another ship further out. "I see Shaw's *Savage of the Sea* is here."

"Aye," Fraser replied. Just as planned.

There was no missing the mighty vessel. One prominent sail, ruddy in color, had a massive ship painted on it with the image of a devil's head with a sword-bearing fist crushing it.

Douglas and Innis knew better than to make any more mention of it as ears were always listening. Yet Shaw was there with good reason. He was part of Fraser's plan. Not only had MacDougall been paid well but he was given a chance to attack a rival. Always a good day for Shaw when that happened. He also suspected MacDougall wouldn't mind avenging Elspeth.

Fraser kept his eyes bored as they drifted to the Scottish brigantine again.

Unbeknownst to most, it had special cargo on it. En route to Dartmouth, its captain was a privateer under special orders from the current Lord High Admiral of England, Henry Holland, third Duke of Exeter. In fact, he carried a Letter of Marque, a document that gave a sailor amnesty from piracy laws as long as the ship's plunder was of an enemy nation.

The cargo itself held little interest to Fraser, but it did to his enemy. Enough so apparently, that Estienne Du Blanc intended to intercept it. More than that, and this is where Shaw MacDougall came in, rumor had it Estienne's allied pirate crew would be there to assist, and that proved too tempting to ignore.

So Shaw had plenty of reasons to fight today including not only a chance to attack his rival but to confiscate extra loot. Not just off the French ships but the Scottish one captained by its womanizing privateer.

"Shaw was right about that one," Douglas noted, not bothering to glance at said privateer, knowing full well he was taking a wench against a tree for all to see. The act wasn't all that uncommon just a rougher, more degrading encounter than most.

The point of the matter was that Shaw had known full well the privateer would not pass this port without stopping off for a romp. While he did, Fraser's wench-turned-spy would use her boundless charms to wrangle information out of the captain's men. Anything new learned could only help Fraser and his comrades.

Then they would be off, following at a discreet distance until the Scottish brigantine, at long last, led him straight to his enemy. A man whose beating heart he would crush with his bare hands.

So he sat back and enjoyed his freshly caught flounder until the time finally arrived.

After the privateer and his crew disembarked, Fraser headed for his ship but not before he spoke with his wench. "Did ye learn anything then, lass?"

"Aye." She looked from the sea back to him, troubled. "Whilst I dinnae know any details, whatever its cargo, 'tis not the sort of treasure ye would expect."

Intrigued, he cocked his head. "If ye dinnae know any details, what upsets ye so?"

"'Twas more what they didnae say that makes me suspect there's foul play afoot." Her stained lips pouted as her eyes leveled with his. "There isnae a pirate in the whole of Britannia that doesnae know ye intend to kill Estienne Du Blanc for the death of yer love." She rested her hand on his forearm, concerned. "Has it not occurred to ye that this might be a trap, Cap'n?"

He had counted on it.

"Och, nay," he scoffed, patting her on the shoulder. "I've looked into this good, lass. Dinnae worry." He leaned close, sure to seem as though he enjoyed her perfumed scent. "For your troubles, ye'll find a little something extra in a pouch behind where I was sitting." His eyes flickered from a boisterous drunk pirate back to her before he winked. "Compliments of the swine who beat ye last week, aye?"

A small smile curled her lips. "If ever ye want to make an honest woman of me, Cap'n MacLomain, I'm all yers."

He met her smile, kissed her cheek, slapped her arse then headed out.

If all went as it should, Estienne Du Blanc would be dead by nightfall.

Chapter Seven

WITHIN THE HOUR, Fraser stood at the helm of his three-mast thirty-eight gun ship, a grand and intimidating prize he had captured a while back. Named *The Sea Rogue* for his exaggerated exploits, she had been an able vessel thus far.

Unlike any boat to date, he bypassed a simple ornamentation on the bow and went one step further. Made to his specifications so it would not overly affect the ship's performance a head structure was built for the front of the craft then a small waist-up figurehead in Elspeth's likeness. Wild and free, she sat proudly on his prow cresting the waves, joining him as he sought out adventure.

She was also a reminder to all who crossed his path that he was out for blood.

Blood that would very soon stain his blade.

He had given Shaw the signal that all was going as planned and the *Savage of the Sea* along with MacDougall's fleet were far enough behind to remain unseen. A fleet, that is, that had remained out to sea, so the Scottish privateer did not spy them.

Innis and Douglas sailed alongside Fraser, just as eager. It would be the three of them Estienne saw when he supposedly commandeered the privateer's brigantine. A ship that was, in all actuality, manned by those who paid their allegiance to Estienne Du Blanc himself.

"It will be good…eh, what is the word…retribution, yes?"

His eyes went to Audric. "Aye, lad, 'twill be good."

As they eventually discovered, Elspeth's young apprentice had unknowingly been at the heart of his mistress's kidnapping. Having been in her inner circle, he had heard things without meaning to. Most specifically, the story of her kin's past and of the MacLauchlin treasure. Thinking it but a tall tale, he had shared it with his grandmother on one of his rare visits home.

Regrettably, what he never could have known was that the tale was based on truth and none other than his own kin were on the other end of that story. Worse yet, that some of those very relatives were pirates. A certain pirate to be exact.

Estienne Du Blanc.

So that is how the enemy learned of Elspeth and her stones.

Stones, as it happened, that Estienne never did get his hands on that fateful night. Though it was rumored he sent men back to search, they were never found.

Convinced that Audric was innocent of any intentional wrongdoing, Fraser tried to send him home, but he refused. Based on his anguish the eve Elspeth was taken and his fierce determination to save her, he would say the boy loved her as much as the rest of them. So Fraser helped him become a man by allowing him to join his crew and seek his vengeance.

Besides, it didn't hurt to have a healer along.

Since then, Audric had filled out, learned English well enough and became Fraser's third mate. Though his pale blond beard was still sparse and his frame more lanky than muscled, he would someday be formidable. He no longer slumped in a corner but stood tall and gazed with pride at the other ships.

"This day we be victorious." Eagerness lit Audric's eyes as he clenched his dagger. "*Un jour pour se souvenir.*"

Fraser clasped his shoulder and nodded, taking his meaning however incorrectly said. "Aye, lad, 'twill most certainly be that."

A slow, sinister smile curled Fraser's lips as they drew closer to the area where Estienne Du Blanc would make his move. Known for dangerous coral reefs depending on the tide, the enemy had timed it just right. It was a smart location to spring a trap because maneuverability became quite tricky.

Yet Fraser had long planned for a moment such as this and had sailed Scotland's coasts aplenty. He'd talked at length with pirates who spent their life off the shores of Britannia and learned everything he could. He poured over nautical maps, then sailed the waters they spoke of in all types of weather, putting their knowledge to the test and learning the shores firsthand. He knew when the tides came and went and how they affected the coastline.

As Innis often said, Fraser was a natural. Born to the sea. Be that as it may, the majority of it came from paying attention, practicing and never allowing himself to get overconfident. If he had learned nothing else, it was that the sea was to be respected as he was but a mere mortal at its whim.

So he knew precisely how to maneuver his ship in this dangerous location as did his comrades. The key now was timing. If he guessed correctly, Estienne would pretend he and his men were attacking the brigantine. That's when the enemy likely surmised Fraser would make his move and strike.

Yet nothing happened quite as expected.

Instead, the brigantine began reefing its sails and slowed.

So Estienne would not bother with a masquerade after all? He would finally face off with Fraser like a real man? Not the pathetic, cowardly wretch he was.

Yet there was no sign of him. Nor was there any sign of Estienne's allied pirate crew.

Strange.

Too strange.

Much like those agonizing moments right before he learned Elspeth had been taken, everything stilled inside him.

Something was wrong.

"Your orders, Cap'n?" his first mate Magnus asked, coming up alongside him, his eyes just as uneasy. He might be gray haired and sea-worn, but he had more know-how and energy than men half his age.

Fraser was about to respond when something began happening aboard the brigantine.

"*Ça ne peut pas être,*" Audric stuttered before he raced to the bow, white-knuckled the railing and narrowed his eyes. "I cannot see correctly."

Eyes narrowed as well, Fraser shook his head in disbelief as a lass was yanked up from below and hauled roughly to the bow. Her hands were tied behind her back, and a burlap sack covered her head. A man held a blade to her neck as his eyes turned and locked with Fraser's despite the distance.

That wasn't what caused Audric's reaction though.

No, his angst came from who she appeared to be. Petite with pre-cisely the same sort of body and hair trailing down under the burlap, she looked eerily like Elspeth herself.

"Cap'n?" Angus repeated. "Your orders?"

He shook his head and tried to ignore his thundering heart. It couldn't possibly be her...could it? Not after all this time. He kept shaking his head, as he struggled to think clearly.

She was long dead.

This was an illusion.

"'Tis a trap," he whispered. "A better laid one than expected." He frowned, unable to tear his eyes from her. "Begin reefing the sails. Slow us down."

"Aye, Cap'n," Magnus replied before he began barking orders to the men and they set to task.

Though Innis' ship slowed too, Douglas was apparently of the opposite mind as he picked up speed.

"Nay, Brother!" Fraser roared and gestured at Magnus to pursue rather than slow.

Innis held back so that he didn't fall into the thick of what was surely an ambush. He would bide his time and attack from the other side.

"Bloody hell," Fraser muttered as he steered carefully and roared more orders to his second and third mates. "Eyes to the water! Watch the reefs." Then he bellowed over his shoulder. "Ready the cannons!"

Just as he figured, the French pirates had appeared and were closing in fast. Now they had the advantage with Douglas hell-bent on saving the lass.

The way in which Estienne had planned this was clever, driving them into the most perilous area while he remained in an easier spot to navigate. More specifically, a better vantage for firing his guns.

Fraser muttered a slew of curses as he focused on the water. Movement became more and more difficult, some spots leaving less than a fathom between the hull and sharp, damaging coral.

"Take the helm and get us closer to the brigantine," he ordered Magnus as he scooped up a bow and arrow. If his man got him close enough, he could shoot an arrow into the enemy's head and be done with this. Or mayhap at least snap some sense into Douglas so the man could see straight again.

Yet it seemed the enemy had one more trick up his sleeve.

Rather than wait any longer, the man holding the lass sliced her throat.

Though somewhere in the back of his mind, Fraser knew it could not possibly be Elspeth, that same still feeling overcame him. The same crippling deadness he had felt when he heard the news of her death. Not a sense of focus by any means, but a lapse in time when he could not think or see straight.

Only one thing got through beyond a haze of resurrected grief.

Estienne Du Blanc had once again outsmarted him by using his vengeance against him. Because within his vengeance was his love for Elspeth. And that was a weakness to be exploited. As he watched the woman's body sink beneath the water, he realized how vulnerable he had always been. Still was.

Not so vulnerable however that he didn't come to attention when a cannon boomed and barely missed his mainmast. That was all it took. That's what pulled him free.

Because without that mast, they were dead in the water.

Everything he had learned snapped into focus as his eyes swept over the sea. In one fell swoop, he gauged the wind speed, their precise location amongst the reefs, the glare of the sun, each and every cloud and when it might block that glare. Most importantly, he took into account the height of the waves.

Fully aware the cannon had come from one of the enemy ships and that Estienne was closing in fast on his stern, he rejoined Magnus. Not surprisingly, after he discreetly relayed his instructions, his first mate narrowed his eyes. While any in their right mind would question Fraser's orders, Magnus had seen him pull off great feats at sea. That paid off now because though his first mate eyed him for another moment, Magnus finally clasped him on the shoulder and nodded before he raced below deck.

Hands on the helm and eyes to the water, Fraser began counting. Three, two, one until the timing was perfect and he roared, "Boom about!" then cranked the wheel hard. His warning gave his lookout in the Crow's Nest just enough time to strap down and the rest of the crew to brace themselves and duck as the ship turned fast and the boom swung.

Not expecting Fraser to make such a bold move in dangerous waters, he heard the roaring ruckus of the enemy's crew as new orders were given. Legs braced, all his weight against the wheel, his gaze narrowed on the man standing at the other helm.

At long last, he locked eyes with his sworn enemy.

As rumor had told, Estienne Du Blanc was a slight man with a thin, greasy mustache and a too-square chin. His forehead was broad and his skin overly smooth considering how far back his long black hair was receded. Even so, there was a sharp intelligence in his beady eyes.

Eyes that were wrought with frustration right now.

Moments later, Fraser's cannons fired broadside.

It was not only a dangerous move on such a tight turn in gusty winds, but some might think a novice one. Mainly because the ship was already heavily lolled. Add the force of the cannons firing off one side and the ship tilted dangerously while at the same time fired inaccurately.

Yet he knew what his vessel was capable of and had one goal in mind. To make Estienne think him an unworthy adversary so he didn't see Fraser's true intentions until it was too late. To that affect, Mac-Dougall and his imposing ships appearing on the horizon just then could not have happened at a more perfect time.

While Estienne's allied pirate crew had indeed shown up with several ships, they didn't have nearly enough to face off with the MacDougall and live. So it came as no surprise when they turned about and hightailed it in the opposite direction.

Innis and Douglas raised their red flags signaling no quarter would be given and were already attacking Estienne's ships. That, in turn, left

Estienne sitting vulnerable as Fraser came about and headed his way.

He would never forget the look on his enemy's face as it dawned on him what Fraser had intended all along. Not to sink him with cannons but fight hand to fist and have his revenge. He would not receive a swift death by drowning but a much slower, more tortuous one at the end of Fraser's jagged-edged blade.

First, though, he would cripple his ship.

Any pirate worth their salt knew better than to attempt to board Fraser's ship with good reason. He had razor sharp crescent blades attached to the outer most edge of his masts. So Estienne knew precisely what Fraser was up to as he loomed closer and closer. Because *The Sea Rogue*'s blades were hellishly long and lethal.

There would be no turning. No getting away.

Fraser had him trapped.

Soon enough, his ship came alongside Estienne's, shredding his sails to bits. Meanwhile, Fraser's men perched on the fighting platforms halfway up the mainmast and foremast began raining down arrows on the enemy's vulnerable crew. Seconds later, *The Sea Rogue*'s gangplank dropped, slamming down on the side of Estienne's ship before Fraser's men roared and began attacking.

Eyes on Estienne, Fraser joined in the fray, slashing down any man that stood in his way. Not truly seeing any he killed he ran his blade across one faceless man's throat before he impaled the next. He tossed one overboard then snapped the neck of another.

All the while, he moved ever closer to the stairs leading to the helm.

All the while, he kept ready the blade that would carve out Estienne's heart.

His pulse raced in sweet anticipation. The moment he had waited seven hundred and forty-two days for had finally arrived. There would be no more sleepless nights as rage consumed him. No more waiting and biding his time as he thought up clever ways to disembowel his enemy.

Unfortunately, he was so bound and determined to at last reap his vengeance that he never saw what hit him when he began bounding up the stairs toward Estienne. Having used the railings on either side to gain momentum, a scrawny boy with a heavy knit cap kicked him hard in the chest.

He staggered, tried to gain his footing but instead landed flat on his back. Mystified that someone had managed to take him down, he peered up, but the glare of the sun made it difficult to see. Frustrated that this half pint had kept him from his prey, his warrior instincts kicked in, and he paid attention to details.

The inexperienced grip the boy had on the hilt of his sword.

How his overly cocky swagger was at odds with the telling furrow of his brow.

This child was a novice. He had gotten lucky with that kick.

It would *not* happen again.

Prepared to take him down quickly, he lurched onto one knee and swept his leg around. Rather than trip and fall, the boy leapt then did his own swift spin and caught Fraser in his shoulder. A blink later, still taking advantage of the sun behind him, the boy's blade nearly got by his defenses, but he intercepted it a mere fraction from his face.

Bloody hell, the lad knew how to fight after all.

Now that he had a better idea of what he faced, he counterattacked, leaping to his feet and intimidating with his height and strength. As his opponent came at him, he paid close attention to the lad's every move. His thrusts were well-timed and perfectly executed as he kept the sun in Fraser's eyes.

Truth told it was the best swordplay he had enjoyed in ages.

As they ducked and swirled around others, the boy not only used the sun to his advantage but various parts of the main deck. With his limber size, he remained one step ahead, maneuvering through things

Fraser had to circumvent. He would use rigging to swing around a mast before he caught him in the chest again. Then he'd scramble back and trip a random fighter who would then barrel into Fraser.

By the time he finally caught up with him, the little rug rat had him in a good rage.

Enjoyable competition or not, he was supposed to be watching Estienne's blood trail down his body from various well-placed slashes. He was supposed to be enjoying the terror in his eyes under Fraser's torturous onslaught. Yet nay, instead he was getting bested by a twig of a boy that barely seemed winded.

Well, no more.

Enough with this nonsense.

With a mighty roar, he attacked him with everything he had. All the fury and heartache he had suffered. Brutal, methodical, he came at the boy so fast he had no chance. Two strikes later, he finally managed to knock the sword from the lad's hand. Before he knew what hit him, Fraser grabbed the front of his tunic, brought him to the deck and whipped out his dagger.

Shaking with rage, he wedged the blade against the lad's neck, ready to swipe, but stopped short. Though he had embraced his berserker and his fury made anything outside of killing hazy, something got through. Something he thought at first must be an illusion as he finally saw the lad's face for the first time.

The stubborn notch of his chin.

The curve of his cheek.

Most especially, the fire in his eyes.

This was no lad but a *lass*.

The lass.

He had been moments away from slaying not the enemy but the love of his life.

As he lived and breathed, his rival was none other than Elspeth MacLauchlin.

Chapter Eight

F OR THE FIRST time in two long years Elspeth once again stared into the eyes that had kept her going. Icy pale blue eyes that she always returned to in her endless, haunted dreams. While she wanted to grab onto him and never let go, she knew she could not.

"Ye have to let Estienne go, Fraser," she whispered as he yanked his blade away and stared at her in wide-eyed disbelief. "Ye've got to let him go, or my kin will die."

Thankfully, fighting was still going on around them so Estienne could not hear.

But he could see.

"Estienne and his kin know where ye moved my village and family," she whispered, trembling as she tried to get through to him. "If he dies at your hand, his father will end them before we make it halfway around Scotland."

When he shook his head, still mute, she tried to get through another way and growled through clenched teeth, "Do ye ken, Cap'n MacLomain? If ye murder Estienne now, ye'll murder everyone I care about." She pleaded with her eyes. "Ye'll murder Da, Ma, Arabel, wee

Greer. All I have left in this world."

That, it seemed, broke the barrier of his stupefaction because he nodded once.

"Good," she whispered and swallowed hard, sure to look afraid. "Now you're going call off your men and leave me behind."

His eyes narrowed at that, and he finally found his voice. "Bloody hell, nay." He shook his head. "I'll not leave ye, lass."

"Ye will," she assured, having adapted a very specific tone when dealing with Estienne. One of authority. "And ye will do it right now."

But of course, Fraser was not Estienne.

His brows slammed together as a scowl ravaged his face. "I willnae."

"Ye will."

"Nay."

"Aye." She shook her head, kept her eyes cold and said what needed saying. "I dinnae love ye anymore, Fraser. I havenae for some time."

For a flicker of a moment, his expression mimicked the one he wore when she kicked him in the chest. But he quickly recovered, not convinced in the least as his doubtful eyes narrowed. "Ye just say that to drive me away."

"I say it because 'tis true." She frowned, not entirely fibbing with her disgusted response. "I've heard about your endless exploits with wenches. How ye might claim to seek vengeance over your long lost love, but it doesnae stop ye from lusting just fine." Her eyes widened. "And in case ye need reminding, such romping was bragged about long before my supposed death."

Granted he had his needs and she was supposedly long gone, but still. If she heard another wench rave in port about the dashing Cap'n Fraser "The Rogue" MacLomain and his powerful and verra stiff mainmast, she was going to slit someone's throat.

Fraser didn't banter with more words but simply kept his eyes narrowed on hers for another too-long moment before he leapt up. For a split second, it appeared he would indeed leave her, but she should have known better. Instead, he flung her over his shoulder, roared for his men to follow and leapt aboard his ship.

All the while she screamed, kicked and punched, but he deflected well.

"Dinnae do this," she seethed softly. "My kin is safer if I stay with him."

"'Tis clear now your kin isnae safe no matter where ye are," he countered. "So you're better off with me."

In a perfect world, yes. But this was not it.

"Stop struggling," he growled.

"Nay," she spat. "If you're determined to be a stubborn swine then I'll at least make it clear I have no wish to go with ye."

She screamed Estienne's name, sure to make the pitch of her voice piercing.

"Ye wee bloody…" Fraser began, muttering more under his breath as he stomped inside, and headed for the captain's quarters of his ship. Still muttering something about her not knowing what was good for her and that this was no way to greet him, he tossed her on his bed.

Elspeth scrambled after him but not fast enough. In the short time it took her to race his way, he yanked a man by a leash after him and slammed the door shut in her face. She tried to tug it open, but it was no use.

He had locked it.

She flew to the long row of windows that lined the back wall and peered out, desperate to see what was happening. Would he do as she asked? Or would he kill Estienne?

"Please dinnae, Fraser," she whispered as she leaned her forehead against the pane and closed her eyes. Her kin were at stake. Surely that would mean something. Surely he would be able to see past his rage and do the right thing.

Though she could view little of what was happening on Estienne's ship, when she opened her eyes again she could see another. Her brother's ship was pulling up alongside theirs. She put a hand over her mouth, fighting emotion as she stared at it.

Douglas.

How she had missed him. How she had missed them all.

Her eyes slowly drifted around the room as it finally sank in that she was no longer aboard the enemy's ship. That she was, without question, the safest she had been in years.

That she was with Fraser again.

Like him, the room was very masculine. A large, sturdy oak desk sat in front of the windows and furnishings were sparse but expensive. Tasteful. She inhaled deeply, drawing in his lingering spicy scent before her eyes landed on a painting across from his desk. It was a remarkable likeness of her in a most unexpected position.

Fresh tears sprang to her eyes as she gazed at it.

In the portrait, she sat in front of the fire as she had in the cave that night. Her head was bent as she gazed at the ring he had made for her. The one he slipped on right before asking her to marry him. While she remembered feeling a great many things at that moment, the look in her eyes bespoke only one thing.

Love.

The woman in that painting had finally met the great love of her life and saw a future she never expected. A fresh beginning. A chance to start over with a new family and mayhap even have another wee bairn. Funny, until she looked at the picture, she didn't realize how hopeful she had been. How naïve despite all she had gone through already.

She wiped away a stray tear, turned from the painting and sighed. She had been foolishly hopeful but knew better now. Dreaming of such things only ended in pain. Because there was always someone out there determined to take it away from you.

Her eyes whipped outside again when the ship began moving. Hands braced on the sill, she prayed to God Fraser had listened. That he hadn't chosen vengeance over her kin. Her heart lurched then stilled as she waited with baited breath.

Was this it?

Was all lost?

Soon enough, they cleared the enemy ship, and she could see.

"Oh, thank ye," she whispered hoarsely.

Estienne's ship was in bad shape with shredded sails, but it remained afloat. More importantly, its captain was alive. When Estienne's gaze found hers, there was no mistaking the masked approval in his eyes. The sinister triumph hidden beneath his purposeful scowl. May God save her soul for her part in that dark conniving look. For aiding such vermin.

She lingered there, watching until the door flung open. Not to Fraser but her brother.

"Elspeth," he whispered, staring at her, dumbfounded. "Is it really ye, lass?"

"Aye," she barely got out before he crossed the room, pulled her into his arms and embraced her tightly.

"I didnae think ye lived…" he whispered then trailed off.

Accustomed to keeping tears well hidden in front of others, she clenched her teeth, fought a wave of emotion and returned his embrace. Eventually, he held her at arm's length and looked her over.

"What happened to ye?" Worry and anger knit his brows. "Did they hurt ye?"

"Nay." She frowned and shook her head. While she wanted to tell him everything, including the urgency of their situation now, she had watched what happened out on the water. She knew her brother could be impetuous if his emotions got the better of him. "I need to talk to Fraser."

She might be aggravated with him right now, but it was clear he was an excellent seaman and a savvy pirate. And that is what she needed right now. Someone who would think well and act decisively.

"Can we not catch up first, Sister?" Douglas asked. "Ye dinnae know what it's been like for me… for all of us."

"We *will* catch up," she assured him, making her voice a little firmer. "But right now I need to speak with Fraser. 'Tis important, Brother."

A heavy frown settled on his face, but he nodded. "Aye, then, Elspeth…but ye should know he's a changed man. He isnae the Fraser ye once knew."

"I heard the rumors, Douglas," she said softly. "I know what he's become."

"I'm not referring to the rumors," he replied. "Half of those were fabricated anyway." He considered her before he confessed to more than Fraser would likely want her to know. "I refer more so to the bitterness that has eaten at him over time. The need to catch an enemy that forever eluded him…the heartache he suffered at your loss."

"Aye, but he saw to that heartache just fine," she muttered.

Her brother eyed her in confusion for a moment before he took her meaning. "Och, ye cannae mean the wenches, aye?"

She shrugged, not about to have a conversation that further entertained petty jealousy.

"'Twas not what ye think betwixt him and the wenches Elspeth," Douglas said. "Aye, like any man with needs, though he might have enjoyed one on occasion, they were but part of the long game he's been playing. A grateful part, I'd say, with fuller purses for it."

She suddenly felt the fool as their eyes held. He was telling the truth.

But of course, he was. This was Fraser they were talking about. No matter how much he might have changed, even in his darkest hour, he would remain noble minded when it came to the innocent. Had he not proven as much in his long pursuit of avenging her? Of seeing her captor brought to justice however ruthless and sinister the reckoning might have been?

Nevertheless, now was not the time to dwell on such things. She had to remain focused.

"I need to speak with him, Douglas," she persisted.

Her brother sighed and eyed her before he finally nodded.

"Aye, then," he muttered. "I'll let him know."

"Thank ye." She embraced him again and then began pacing after he left.

Anxious, she tried to sort out how to word things. How to keep her emotions under wrap as she shared information that would surely test Fraser's patience even further. She had to do it though. For those she cared about. So she breathed deeply several times, straightened her shoulders and reassured herself that he was just another man and that she could handle him.

Yet when the door finally opened, and he stood there, his eyes brooding as they locked on hers, she remembered all too well that Fraser was *not* just another man. Though she thought it impossible, life at sea clearly agreed with him, and he was even fiercer and more handsome than she remembered.

He wore the MacLomain plaid she had fixed for him, black boots, a white tunic and a bandana wrapped around his head. Bearded now with far more small braids interwoven in his hair, tattoos etched his sun darkened skin. Any gauntness he might have suffered from his illness years ago was long gone. If anything, he seemed more muscular and imposing.

Neither said a word for several moments as he closed the door and they continued eying one another. He had a way of filling a room no matter how large it was. A way of being all around her though he still stood several feet away. For a flicker of a moment, she saw raw pain in his eyes, but it soon vanished, to be replaced with a hardened look that hadn't been there before.

Douglas was right. He had changed.

But not in some ways. Not in how he felt about her. That had been clear when he, at last, recognized her. The surge of disbelief then joy before she had doused the reunion with harsh words.

"Tell me what happened, Elspeth," he finally ground out. He remained where he was, his fists clenched, and his body tight as his eyes stayed on hers. "Tell me all of it."

She would. At least what he needed to know.

So she led with information that would diffuse his anger rather than ignite it. "I was never raped or hurt in any way."

Hurt beyond repair that is.

"Rather, I was taken by Estienne for a verra specific reason," she continued. "Of course, because I had knowledge of the stones and treasure but also to see to his wounded father, André. A vicious and dangerous man indeed."

Fraser remained silent and went to a side cabinet for whisky as she continued.

"I saved André's life," she said. "In exchange, rather than give me to his men, he gave me to Estienne. 'Twas more of an indulgence than anything. Someone to make a man out of him, entertain him and heal him if he was wounded." She shook her head. "For that, I remained safe from Estienne's crew as well."

Fraser handed her a mug of whisky, his lips a grim line, his voice low and dangerous. "And did ye make a man out of him, lass? Did ye entertain him?"

"Rest assured, I wasnae his type if ye take my meaning," she replied. "But aye, I entertained him well enough with my wit." She remembered all too well the sleepless nights formulating her next interesting tale. Thankfully, she was not new to storytelling. Such a thing had often helped keep her patients' mind off their pain. "So whether or not I was in the mood, I became someone worth listening to no matter how tall my tale. I made sure to befriend him."

Or at least keep him mildly amused.

"And this?" He fingered her hat before his eyes slowly roamed down her loosely clad body.

She had almost forgotten what it felt like to feel his gaze. The way it tore down her defenses. How heat fired beneath her skin from one smoldering look.

"This clothing was freedom," she said softly as she pulled off the knit cap. "After nearly half a year of being tucked away in his cabin, I finally convinced Estienne that I needed inspiration so that my stories remained intriguing." She set aside the hat and raked a hand through her shoulder-length locks. "I needed the sea and life and people to infuse me. I needed fodder for a good story."

"So ye became a pirate," Fraser murmured, stepping a wee bit closer."

"Aye, 'twas the only way Estienne would allow it," she replied. "I was not to entice his men. So I cut my hair, wrapped my chest, dressed appropriately and embraced piratehood as only a young, adventuresome lad could."

The look in his eyes when they fell to her wrapped chest bespoke a man remembering well what lay beneath the material. Or had *almost* known. She took a hearty swig of whisky not only to distract him but to soothe her suddenly dry throat.

Changed or not, the man still made her heart race.

"Though Estienne's crew already knew he had a lass on board, it was still a period of adjustment when I began working aboard the ship," she went on, trying not to flinch as she recalled those first few months. "'Twas at that time, rumors were spread that I'd been killed. This made wandering eyes less likely to see Cap'n Fraser MacLomain's missing lass when they looked my way." She slanted him a look. "Or should I say, see the bountiful loot ye were willing to offer for my safe return."

"I would have paid anything," he murmured, his eyes on hers, his focus fully on what she had endured. "Tell me about this period of adjustment ye suffered when first becoming a pirate."

She should have known he would not let that slip by unaddressed.

"'Twas as it would have been for any lass in such a position." While tempted to step away because his proximity made thinking difficult, she did not. "But I learned how to handle myself." Did she ever. It was not only a matter of avoiding rape but even death at times. "No eye contact and certainly no feminine actions of any sort." She notched her chin, proud of how far she had come. "I learned to sail well, fight better and thieve as good as the lot of them."

"Aye." Despite his aggravation, she swore a twinkle lit his eyes. "And I see ye remembered what I taught ye."

"I did." He was referring to her initial method when they battled on Estienne's ship. If she was going to act the novice, do so well. "'Twas good advice and helped me on more than one occasion."

Actually, it had saved her life.

"And what of the stones?" He fingered a lock of her hair, his eyes lingering on it as though he feared he might be dreaming. "What of the MacLauchlin's great treasure?"

"Ye tell me," she murmured, watching him closely. "Because the stones werenae where I left them."

His eyes shot to hers. "Ye went back to our cave?"

"I had no choice," she whispered, doing her best to keep the pain from her eyes and voice. "The lives of everyone I cared about were threatened…your life was threatened."

It didn't matter how ferocious the tales were of him battling at her village that fateful day. How powerful he was. He was still a man and men could bleed. Men could die.

"Yet ye were not killed when ye came up empty handed," he said.

"And I havenae been killed since nor have your kin or people."

This is where she needed to be careful.

Where she needed to begin putting her plan in motion. A plan she wasn't sure she could see through.

"My kin havenae been hurt yet." She frowned and shook her head. "But now, because of your actions, they are in dire trouble. My servitude is all that stood betwixt their safety and certain death."

"Are ye sure they know where your people are?" Fraser met her frown. "Could they not have been tricking ye?" He shook his head. "Because we hid them well just south of the Isle of Scarba as your parents and Douglas insisted. They remain under the watchful eyes of Shaw's crew and mine as well when we happen through."

She narrowed her eyes. "That's close to our kin's original land."

"'Tis." He nodded. "And 'tis far closer to the *Devils of the Deep*'s home base. Far safer than anywhere on the east coast of Scotland right now."

"'Tis also far too close to where the treasure supposedly is." She scowled, wishing she had managed to wrangle this information out of Estienne sooner.

"Aye, 'tis verra close to where the treasure was," he said. "Where they thought Estienne might eventually bring ye in hopes ye had memorized those stones."

When his fingers trailed down the side of her neck, a shiver rippled through her, and her breath caught. She couldn't help but close her eyes. It had been so long since she felt this. So long since she felt how he could affect her with the slightest touch.

"Ye lied," he whispered, even closer now.

"About what," she whispered, her eyes still closed as she sunk into the moment. As she feared she might open them again and he would be gone. It would be yet another dream.

"Ye lied about not loving me anymore."

Of course, she had. Every word of it.

"Nay," she whispered because she knew, in the end, it wouldn't matter.

"Aye." She felt a little tug at the back of her neck. "And I'm more than ready to hear the answer to the question I asked ye so long ago."

Her eyes opened to the damning evidence she had forgotten to hide. What she had kept with her every day since she last laid eyes on him. Something that she had stared at every evening before she drifted off to sleep. That kept her strong when she was barely hanging on.

Something she now wore around her neck.

The ring he had given her the night she was taken.

Chapter Nine

I T HAD TAKEN a great deal of strength not to pull Elspeth into his arms as soon as he returned to his cabin. He did not believe she no longer loved him. Not for a moment. And now he had his proof.

The ring.

Rather than give her a moment to deny or even answer his question, Fraser yanked her against him and kissed her hard. He had been desperate to do this since the second he laid eyes on her. Hell, long before that in his haunted dreams.

She was alive.

Here.

In his arms.

Though she stiffened at first, it wasn't long before she melted against him and returned his kiss with as much fervor. Their tongues wrapped and tangled as he brushed aside scrolls and propped her on the edge of his desk.

He wanted to pick up where they left off two years ago.

To feel her sweet heat and finally make her his.

Eager, desperate, he braced himself against the roll of the ship, deepened the kiss and slid his hand up beneath her tunic. With a few swift tugs, he yanked away the material that had bound her breasts and tossed aside the bloody thing. Gone were the days she was anything but his lass. Gone were the days she was some 'lad' facing endless danger.

She groaned in pleasure and spread her thighs as he palmed the soft flesh of one rounded breast before he rolled the pert nipple between his thumb and forefinger. When her head fell back in submission, he yanked his tunic off then nibbled his way down the side of her neck as he ground against her.

She tasted of sea and salt and all the wildness he knew she possessed.

He could feel the burning heat of anticipation between her legs. She was as ready for him as he was for her. In fact, he was long past ready to slip into the sweet bliss that awaited him between her trembling thighs. Painfully desperate and beyond impatient, he yanked at her trouser's strings moments before a loud knock came at the door.

"Cap'n, yer needed on deck," Magnus called out.

"Handle it," he roared, intending to enjoy Elspeth's wee body first.

Or so he had hoped until he realized it was too late. It seemed the blasted interruption had stolen the moment because much to his dismay, she wiggled free.

"Och, lass," he muttered, his cock hard as steel. He needed release. Now. Inside *her*.

"'Tis not a matter that can wait," Magnus continued. "'Tis something that needs yer way with words, Cap'n."

"Bloody hell," he muttered as he stepped away and yanked on his tunic. "The one time my quartermaster isnae bloody with me!"

Had he been, Elspeth would not be putting that God-awful hat back on but spread across his desk with her legs wrapped around him.

"Stay here, lass," he muttered before he strode out. Though it was more of a request, it became a flat out order when he decided to lock her in again. He didn't need her causing a stir with his men.

As it turned out and not surprisingly, his crew was in an uproar over the lack of loot. Not only had they been ordered to abandon Estienne's ship and possible coin, but the two ships they confiscated had next to nothing on them.

Shaw and his crew were gone. While glad to hear of Elspeth's safe return, he had other things to attend to and was already well compensated for his time.

"We've two ships to sell now," Fraser declared as he took to the helm and gave them his undivided attention. "I'll see the proceeds divided evenly amongst ye."

"Och, Cap'n, have ye *looked* at the ships?" one man called out. "Cap'n Douglas took out his foul mood on one of 'em."

Fraser eyed the dilapidated vessel and sighed. That he had.

"Aye and Cap'n Innis got out his aggravation too," another called, gesturing at the other ship.

He crossed his arms over his chest and eyed the other one. It was almost worse than the first.

"We'll take what we can scrap," Fraser finally said after some consideration. "Then I'll see ye compensated some other way."

"What other way, Cap'n?" a third man called out, his eyes narrowed on Fraser as he picked food out of his teeth with the end of a small dagger.

"I'll figure it out," he assured. And he would.

"How 'bout the way the lad's sayin'?" the man replied.

"What lad?" asked another. "And what's he sayin'?"

"The lad yellin' out the window from the captain's quarters." He pointed over his shoulder with his thumb, referring to the windows beneath him. "My guess is the one the cap'n brought on board." He resumed peering at Fraser with a narrowed eye. "He's sayin' he knows where there's treasure the likes of which we've never seen."

Elspeth.

Bloody hell. The lass would be the death of him. He tossed his cabin key to Magnus and gave him a look that said deal with it. Specifically, keep her away from the windows and her mouth shut.

"That true, Cap'n?" the man continued. "Ye know where there's treasure?" He spit out dislodged food. "'Cause I'd hate to think yer holdin' out on us."

"Och," another lad muttered. "Cap'n MacLomain doesnae hold out on his men, ye bastard."

The man who had accused him of such was newer to the crew but not altogether wrong.

Had he half the wit he usually did, Fraser would have stuck to getting answers out of Elspeth rather than ending up between her thighs. He had yet to fully explain her presence to his men but he would. All they knew right now was that she had been important to Estienne and her being taken by Fraser was part of their enemy's torture.

That was part of the reason he gave for leaving Estienne stranded after all his men were killed. The main reason being that Fraser felt a slower death more satisfying after all. A pitiful demise by dehydration and starvation.

He knew many found his change of heart curious considering his long-standing vendetta, but they knew better than to question him. Or at least they did until now.

Until her.

His crew eyed him suspiciously as Elspeth apparently kept feeding information to the scoundrel closest to her. If nothing else had become clear, she had Fraser cornered. And all because he had not taken the time to get the answers he needed but put lusting before captaining.

Either way, he had no intention of backing her claim of treasure. It was too risky until he had all the facts. For all he knew, it might very well be a trap. He was about to say as much when he was interrupted by an all-too-familiar voice.

"Och, nay, yer cap'n isnae holding out on ye," Elspeth declared as she swaggered out. "He just didnae have his facts straight yet is all." Her eyes swept over his men as she headed Fraser's way. "But I *do* have all the facts, and I know precisely where the treasure is!" Her eyes rounded on them, her voice infused with awe. "Treasure the likes ye couldnae imagine!"

Fraser crossed his arms over his chest and eyed her with a heavy frown as she joined him.

"Where is Magnus?" he growled out of the corner of his mouth.

Her telling eyes dropped boldly to his groin before she winked and shrugged. "In a wee bit o' pain at the moment but in a few minutes he should be just fine."

"Och," he muttered and shook his head. "Ye play a dangerous game, lassie."

"Aye." She grinned. "'Tis the way of a pirate."

About to drag her back to his cabin before she caused more damage, she took the possibility out of his hands when she made an even bolder move.

"I know of treasure because 'tis my kin's," she declared to his crew as she ripped off her hat and shook out her hair. "And 'tis the verra reason the enemy stole me away two years ago and your good cap'n has been out for revenge ever since!"

A stunned silence fell as men undoubtedly recognized her from *The Sea Rogue's* figurehead and likely from the portrait in his cabin.

"Bloody hell!" someone finally spoke up. "'Tis Elspeth MacLauchlin arisen from the dead!"

The ship rumbled with a mix of mutterings and roars of approval before they quieted under a glare of warning from their captain. The last thing he needed, no matter how well she could handle herself, was a lass on board. Especially one as beautiful as her. She might be dressed like a lad with her hair sticking up at odd angles, but there was no denying her sun-kissed beauty.

He didn't need to raise his voice when he spoke to his crew. His warning came through loud and clear.

"Aye, she's Elspeth MacLauchlin, my long lost lass." His narrowed eyes went from man to man. "As such, she's not to be touched or even looked at the wrong way, ye ken?"

There were plenty of 'aye Cap'n's' before the man with the food in his teeth leered, chuckled and said, "Och, he'll tire of her eventually then…"

That's all he got out before Fraser whipped a dagger at him followed by someone else's knife. The man froze as both blades thumped into the mizzen mast beside him, one above the other. They were so close to his face that they left two scratches on his cheek.

Fraser arched a brow at Elspeth, impressed with her aim despite his current aggravation. "Good throw."

She grinned. "Ye too."

The crew's incredulous eyes went back and forth between the man and Fraser and Elspeth before their victim managed to speak. "She's yer lass, all right, Cap'n!" His eyes rounded as he eyed the blades then looked Elspeth's way again. "And ye'd be a bloody fool to *ever* tire of the likes of her!"

"Aye," the crew roared, nodding their approval.

"Aye, *féroce*…ferocious," Audric kicked in, stars in his eyes as he gazed at her. "A true tiger female!"

Elspeth smiled warmly at him and nodded hello. Of course, doing such magnified her beauty which had most of his crew looking at her with the same stars in their eyes. Respectful somewhat non-lustful stars that is.

She had swiftly established a standing with his men and saved him from future issues with them. As such, she seemed quite pleased with herself. And she should be. He would give her that…and so much more. Because while she had certainly made it obvious to his crew where she stood, so had he.

She was his.

Therefore, much to her vexation, he didn't hesitate to wrap his arm around her shoulders and pull her against his side. He could tell by her tight expression, that she was not pleased by his public display. One that tested her well-earned independence. But she deserved a little payback for claiming there was a treasure when he knew full well there might not be.

Furthermore, she had bypassed him on his own ship to get what she wanted.

Not to say he didn't want to keep her kin safe. He most certainly did. But there had been no time to assess the situation. She had given him no chance to agree or disagree with her but took matters into her own hands. He conveniently set aside that he had given her little opportunity once he kissed her.

"So where's this treasure, then?" one of his men called out. "And if the enemy took ye to find it why hasnae he found it?"

"Because he doesnae have the treasure map," she explained, nudging her shoulder against Fraser a bit to try to get him to loosen his hold. She proceeded to tell them the same story she had told him in his cabin about Estienne and André. "So ye see there is danger to be had if we seek it out, but if ye help me and my kin, I will give ye your fair share."

"I've never heard of Estienne's da, André Du Blanc," a crewmember replied before he chuckled and mocked Estienne's abandoned-at-sea-status. "Is he as much of a threat as his son, then?"

Fraser figured she would downplay how threatening she found André to get them to do what she wanted, but she didn't. Rather, she was honest, and it appeared they appreciated it based on the look in their eyes.

"I havenae seen André fight, but I've heard rumor he's verra good," she said bluntly. "And he leads a wicked crew." Her eyes went from man to man as she gave it to them straight. "Yet he has a weakness and 'twas clear when I was forced to nurse him back from the brink of death."

"And what is that?" the man with the dagger asked.

"His son, Estienne," she replied. "'Tis why we left him alive. Had we not, André's wrath would have been formidable not only on my people but on all of ye." Her eyes swept over them in warning. "Because if André possesses nothing else, 'tis a long memory."

Fraser didn't need to ask to know André was at the root of all this. *He* was the one who kept the tale of the MacLauchlin treasure alive. *He* was the one who ordered the attack on her village years ago…the one who saw her husband killed and her child taken.

Which made him wonder if Audric's placement with Elspeth wasn't planned all along. Not by the lad. He didn't have it in him. But by an enemy that had begun figuring things out long ago.

"So now the cap'n has stolen ye back," another crewmember continued, his eyes on Elspeth as he apparently felt the need to recap. "Which I cannae say I blame him despite the risk to yer family." He tilted his head at the ship's figurehead, reminding her of what a valued prize she really was. "But taking ye means hell to pay 'cause André will see through his threat and attack yer kin, aye?"

"That's right," she confirmed. "So I need ye to harness the substantial courage I know ye have and defend them alongside me." Her rallying speech took a serious turn. "If ye do I'll make ye verra wealthy indeed." She nodded, her performance very convincing. "Ye have my word. 'Twill be a prize well worth fighting for."

"So ye say," Magnus groused as he limped out, his groin clearly tender. "But where is this treasure map?"

"In Argyll." Her gaze was as level as her words. "Hidden close to the village." She gave them a telling look. "And only I know how to find it."

"'Tis a wonder André didnae force such information out of ye sooner," Magnus remarked dryly.

Fraser's thoughts exactly.

"But he did," she said softly. Her eyes avoided Fraser's as she turned and lifted the back of her tunic, exposing the angry welts where lashes had struck the tender flesh across her shoulder blades and lower back.

Bloody *hell*.

Red hot fury blazed through him at the sight. At what she had suffered. Forget revenge on just Estienne Du Blanc. His father would also burn in an eternal Hell of Fraser's making.

"This is what happened to me when I didnae lead André to the treasure," she informed them, her eyes still bypassing Fraser's as she lowered her shirt and faced off with his men. "Ye see André *did* threaten my village if I didnae give up the map." She shrugged. "And that might have happened had his son Estienne not wanted me as his healer." She shook her head. "And everyone knows André denies his son nothing." The corner of her mouth curled up. "So I had my leverage."

"The whole of Britannia knew your good cap'n was out for vengeance," she continued. "That he would stop at nothing to have it." Deviousness lit her eyes. "So in exchange for my people's safety, I told André I would make sure Fraser didnae kill his son when he finally caught up with him."

She shook her head, sad and remorseful. "Now, however, 'tis only a matter of time before André makes his move on my village."

Only Fraser seemed to see the manipulative light in her eyes as she again looked from man to man and sprung her trap. "Now I'm afraid the enemy will get to the treasure before us." Her brows swept up in resignation. "After all, my parents know where 'tis hidden." She pressed her lips together, woeful. "And I can tell ye with certainty, that if their bairns' lives are threatened, they willnae hesitate to share."

Chapter Ten

SEVERAL HOURS LATER, as they sailed up the eastern shores of Scotland she sat across a small table from Fraser in his cabin. Water slapped the sides of the hull and lanterns swung back and forth as the ship lolled.

They had just finished eating, and Fraser had barely said a word. Rather, he appeared to be stewing in thoughts she imagined had to do with her swindling his crew into going on a treasure hunt.

While relieved she had swayed them, her guilt only grew every moment that passed. Was she doing the right thing? Would she be able to come up with a more concrete plan before they arrived? Would she be able to save him?

"I believe ye think even darker thoughts than me," Fraser finally said, his voice deceptively soft, his eyes caught in the shadows. Though his demeanor appeared casual enough, she knew he watched her closely. Almost like a predator stalking their prey.

"My thoughts are my own," she murmured as her eyes met his. "I willnae apologize for my actions today, Fraser. Ye left me no choice."

"Ye gave me no time to leave ye a choice," he countered. Though frustration furrowed his brow, his gaze was gentler than expected. "Ye assumed I wouldnae let ye risk your life again and you're right. At least in those initial moments after I knew ye still lived." He shook his head. "Had ye just given me time, ye have to know I would have done anything for ye, lass. Anything at all."

"I know," she whispered, not quite meeting his eyes now. "I've just become used to a certain way of life. A certain type of people." She clenched her jaw, embracing the unfailing grit she lived by now. "I tend to take what I need rather than wait and let it slip through my fingers." Her eyes returned to his. "I take what I need so I appear strong, not weak."

Silence fell as he considered that. As he likely contemplated what it would have been like to live amongst Estienne's crew for the past two years. But then she imagined he had been doing that since the moment he knew she still lived. Nay, far longer considering the road he had traveled since they last met. The lengths he was willing to go for her.

"Though I might not have liked how ye went around me," he said eventually. "Ye *did* give me renewed faith in what had to have been a verra dark time for ye. 'Tis no doubt ye earned the respect of all around ye and remained safer with Estienne's crew than ye might have otherwise."

Strained silence settled again before he continued. His voice was lower now, thick with repressed angst. "Yet ye didnae escape completely unscathed." His turbulent, disgusted eyes stayed with hers. "I cannae tell ye how sorry I am for what ye suffered at the hands of André Du Blanc." A muscle leapt in his jaw, and he clenched his fists as if eager to strike his enemy. "'Tis a bloody wonder ye survived."

It truly was. She would never forget the blinding pain of being whipped. The endless blood. But she had never given up. Not through the long hours when infection set in. Not when she knew full well she was at death's door.

"'Twas ye and my daughter that got me through," she whispered without meaning to. She cleared her throat and skirted around the whole truth. "I taught one of André's wenches how to care for me. What poultices were necessary." She offered a nod of acknowledgement. A platonic display of thanks. "And I thought of ye and your strength. It inspired me to stay strong through the worst of it."

While in reality, that was true, it went deeper. Far deeper.

His gaze sharpened at the particular octave of her voice when she mentioned her daughter. His words were measured and careful when he spoke. "'Tis good that thoughts of your wee one helped ye through."

It was clear he knew there was more to this than she was saying.

"Aye." Though it was hard to speak of it, she found herself sharing more than intended. "'Twas indeed Estienne's crew that raided my village so long ago. 'Twas his men that killed my husband and took my daughter." She shook her head. "Even then he took his orders from André who had them raiding villages up and down the coast." She tempered emotion when it tried to surface. "It was me calling out my daughter's full name that night that alerted André to our presence there."

His expression darkened as she continued.

"As ye know, after that raid, Douglas and Innis embraced piratehood and swore allegiance to the *Devils of the Deep*," she said. "Shaw MacDougall's name alone made attacking the village again far riskier, so André took a different approach and exercised a great deal of patience."

Fraser quickly put the pieces together. "Though the lad didnae know it, André sent Audric to ye with a purpose."

"Aye," she confirmed. "An innocent boy who I suspect never volunteered information to his grandmother but had it cleverly manipulated out of him. Meanwhile, André bided his time, formulated a plan and waited for the perfect opportunity to take me."

"Bided his time indeed," he murmured, no doubt referring to the great length of time that passed between raids.

"Aye," she said softly, in no mood to elaborate.

Though Fraser's gaze continued to darken hope sparked in his eyes. "And your daughter? Does she live?"

She swallowed hard and set aside emotions once more.

"At first André claimed she was still alive and used her survival as a means to force me to find the treasure." She shook her head. "But even if I had the stones memorized that information was useless without finding the ruins of MacLauchlin Castle."

"Because that is the precise location ye need to stand for the stones to lead the way," he supplied softly putting two and two together.

"Aye," she confirmed, detached because she had to be when she spoke of this. "In his rage, he confirmed my daughter's death to dishearten and demoralize me then nearly whipped me to death so that my physical pain matched that of my mind and heart."

His jaw clenched, and his nostrils flared. "Ye believed him about your daughter's death then? Truly?"

"Not at first…I remained hopeful." She pressed back against emotion yet again, refusing to feel it. She had separated herself from it long ago. Or so she thought. "'Twas the wench that saw to my wounds who verified his words, claiming her own sister had seen to my child before she met an untimely death."

Silence fell as he clearly struggled with her news. What she had endured. How unkind Fate had been.

"I'm so sorry, lass," he finally said softly.

"'Tis all right," she lied. "I had long accepted that 'twas a possibility and found some comfort in knowing it was over for her. That she was finally at peace."

The truth of it was the news defeated her, and she welcomed death after André whipped her. She would rather have joined her daughter in the afterlife. Yet something kept her going. Kept her from giving up. Not just the growing need to avenge her daughter but the man she would leave behind.

Fraser.

In the throes of fever, she was with him again in her mind. They were back in the cave. Then on the shore. Then she was in his arms when they danced in the village. A constant presence that helped her stave off death, he never left her side. He urged her to keep going. Inspired her to live.

Now, look at what she was about to do to him.

The set-up he didn't see coming.

Not yet anyway.

Her eyes went to her portrait. To the woman she once was. The love in her eyes.

She would never have done what Elspeth was doing now. She would have *never* betrayed the man she loved.

"Ye should do away with that portrait," she said softly, unable to look at it anymore. "It doesnae portray me verra well."

Though it did. At least who she once was.

"I'm sorry ye dinnae like it, lass." His eyes never left her face. "I painted ye just as I remembered ye that eve."

Surprised, her eyes returned to his. "*Ye* painted it?"

"Aye." He shrugged, humble. "It seems I'm a wee bit artistic."

She nodded in agreement thinking of the ring he had made for her. Though tempted to touch it as she always did, she refrained. She didn't want to give him hope where there might not be any. Yet as their eyes held, it felt like hope was sparking to life anyway. That it was unavoidable and destined despite the wayward paths they had traveled.

She wondered though...*did* he have a chance to follow another path? *Could* he have returned to a better life than piracy?

Curious, she asked as much. "Have ye remembered more about

yourself then? More about your kin and your life before I found ye?"

"I have," he replied. "All of it."

Truly? Excited, she sat forward and rested her elbows on the table. "And?"

"Let's just say 'twas far more than I anticipated," he murmured. "And that in many ways I was thrust from one curse into another the moment I lost ye."

"Och." She took a swig of whisky and kept eying him. "So who were ye battling? Who left ye for dead?"

"It doesnae matter now," he said. "It hasnae for some time."

She frowned, not satisfied with that answer. "How vague!" She shook her head. "What of your clan? Have ye gone to visit them? Have ye learned of your position amongst them?"

"I've seen them here and there," he assured, as evasive as ever. "I am not a chieftain nor am I married." One brow crawled up slowly. "Which leads me back to a question ye've yet to answer, lass."

"Ye think to worry about that when ye keep so much from me?"

"Well, I can either focus on that." He shifted forward ever-so-slightly, like a panther ready to pounce. "Or I can focus on all that *ye* continue to keep from *me*."

Hell and damnation, he knew she kept secrets.

Mayhap even suspected that she was setting him up.

"I dinnae know what ye mean," she said.

"Aye, ye do."

"Nay," she insisted.

"Aye."

"Nay."

Their eyes narrowed on one another at the same time.

"Aye, ye *do*," he said, his tone final.

"Think what ye will then," she spat then snapped her mouth shut. It was clear her words fell on deaf ears. Whether those words were true or not was neither here nor there. Not when he got her riled up like this.

Some women might think him especially callous right now considering the news she just shared, but she wasn't one of them. She knew his heart ached for her and her daughter, but that wasn't the matter at hand. Nay, his intolerance for lies fueled his current disposition. More pointedly, if she were to guess, the sort of lies that risked her safety.

Be that as it may, she would not be revealing any hidden truths in her current mood. If ever. The fact she was even wavering on it now frustrated her. She needed to keep a calm, collected mind. Not let him wheedle information out of her.

Their resolute gazes remained locked as silence fell once again. The lanterns cast his face in and out of shadows, adding to the ominous and unpredictable set of his expression.

"It may not be now, but I'll get my answers, lass," he ground out in warning. "When I do, ye will get yours."

She crossed her arms over her chest, scowled and muttered, "Ye really have changed, Fraser MacLomain."

"As have ye," he bit back. "Ye wear my ring so 'tis clear ye still love me." He shook his head, baffled, his temper obviously getting the better of him. "Yet here ye sit lying to me when ye could bloody well be in my bed where ye belong!"

Where she *belonged*? As if it were her place to be on her back with her legs spread.

"And here I thought I belonged on your bloody desk!" she snapped as she launched to her feet.

He might have her pegged about lying, but she did *not* have to tolerate his crass words. Though it was the hardest thing she had ever done, she ripped the ring off and slammed it down on the table. "And the only reason I kept this was for financial security lest I found myself in a position only a pretty bauble might get me out of!"

When she went to storm by him, he caught her elbow. "Where do ye think you're going?"

"Out for some fresh air." She yanked her arm away. "'Tis too oppressive in here."

Sure to slam the door as she left, she yanked on her hat out of habit and slumped her shoulders a little as she stepped around coiled rigging and headed for the bow. Though she had made headway with his crew, it was best to remain cautious and not tempt Fate. With that thought in mind earlier, she had seen to the man's cheek she and Fraser's blades had nicked. Best that the men favor her rather than start doubting her.

Flickering lanterns hung port and starboard as an old salt lounged around and played his hornpipe from a platform on the foremast. Others meandered about, some humming along, some tapping their feet as they swigged whisky.

The moon was wide and full, sparkling over the dark sea as she clenched the railing and tried to calm her emotions. For all the long nights such as this dreaming of the day she would stand aboard Fraser's ship, she found no satisfaction. Though she knew what she intended to do was for the greater good, so much could go wrong.

Yet in her selfishness, she had hatched this plan, then the tides had been turned on her. She had been outmaneuvered by André. Outsmarted at her own game. Now she needed to *think*. To outwit him in return.

"It is a night of beautiful, yes? *Oui*?" came Audric's voice before he appeared out of the darkness beside her. "*Qu'on se souvienne.*"

She flinched at his last words. A night to remember? Mayhap under different circumstances.

"*Qu'on se souvienne,*" she replied, pretending to agree. "'Tis good to see ye again, my friend." She offered a warm smile before she embraced him. "Ye have grown much and traveled a different path than intended, aye?"

He nodded, his eyes worried as she pulled away.

"I know everything," she confirmed, determined to put his mind at ease. "And ye dinnae need to be sorry." She shook her head. He was not to be faulted for his kin's actions. For André's greedy ambition and murderous ways. "I agree with Cap'n Fraser and believe ye were innocent of any wrongdoing."

Audric nodded, plainly fighting emotion as he slumped with relief. "I am so sorry regardless. I am related to some…" He struggled to find the right words. "*Hommes méchants*…evil men."

"One evil man," she corrected. "But rest assured, the enemy's actions dinnae reflect on ye, Audric. Ye arenae anything like André Du Blanc, ye ken?"

Not to say Estienne was any prize either. He was rotten, spineless and deserving of death. He just wasn't quite as demonic as his da. Not yet anyway.

Audric offered a jerky nod, clearly appreciative of her reassuring words. Even so, a frown remained settled on his face as he stood beside her and eyed the sea. "This André will be very unhappy to lose you, yes?"

"Verra," she lied.

"He must be very hateful of the cap'n," he said. "A man determined to put death to his son."

"Aye," she confirmed.

"A man who knew your family secrets as well as I," Audric remarked softly.

Her eyes slid his way. "Aye."

"A man who knew where you kept those stones."

"Ye knew where I kept them too," she murmured, curious to see where the lad was going with this.

"I went back for them with a…" he struggled to find the right words again, "in a deep hope I could give them to my kin in exchange for you." His suspicious eyes met hers. "Yet they were not there."

Though he acted the part of someone perplexed, it was clear he was anything but. He had a theory, and she suspected she knew what it was.

"My brother knew where the stones were too," she reminded. "And my parents."

"True," he conceded. "But none made it to the cave before me that night." His voice remained soft. "Only one man was on the shore trying to get you back the eve you were taken. Only one man had the time to get there before me." He cocked his head. "But I think you already know that."

She narrowed her eyes and played dumb. "What are ye trying to say?"

But she knew. He surmised Fraser had the stones. Moreover, he suspected she was aware of that.

Instead of answering and continuing a conversation which heavily implied she plotted against Fraser, he approached from a different angle.

"Have you heard tales of what happened after you were taken?" He stared at the sea again, his gaze hard to read. "Of Cap'n Fraser's actions?"

"Aye," she replied. "He embraced his rage and turned pirate."

"Rage was the least of it," he murmured as his eyes returned to hers. "There was also…" he searched for words again, "a great deep sadness the likes of which I have never seen. A man who seemed to have lost his very soul." His brows pinched together. "Yet before all else, before the fury that consumed him, he saw to what he knew would be your wishes. Your family's well-being."

"I heard that was Douglas' doing," she said.

"He helped." Audric shook his head. "But 'twas Fraser who thought with a clear head and got them to safety. Who moved them across the whole of Scotland, setting aside his grief whilst he pacified your sisters and distraught parents." Sadness reflected in his eyes. "'Twas *he* who held little Greer every night until she drifted off to sleep, her tears at last dry."

She looked to the ocean again and blinked away moisture. Those tales had not reached her ears and with good reason. Fraser had likely made sure of it because it would have crushed her. He had made sure of many things it seemed.

"He blamed himself as much as I did for them being able to steal you away," Audric divulged. "And has been punishing himself ever since."

"But 'twas not your fault," she whispered. "Neither of your faults."

Audric offered no response to that but kept praising Fraser. It was clear he had a great deal of respect for him. It was also clear he was getting at something. Soon enough, that something became evident.

"There is nothing Cap'n Fraser would not do for you, Elspeth." His eyes remained on the water. "Nothing he would not do to keep you and yours safe." He paused for a moment before his gaze finally settled on her. "Trust in that, yes? Trust in *him*."

Rather than answer, she continued staring into the darkness. Having said his piece, Audric didn't linger much longer but nodded goodnight and left. She didn't have to wonder what he meant by his heartfelt request. Like Fraser, he knew she wasn't honest, and her reasons for being on the ship were nefarious. That said, might she consider being truthful? Might she reveal the secrets they knew she kept from them?

She continued staring at the stars as she often did. Wondering like a fool if they would somehow, someday lead to a happy ending. If there would ever be a light at the end of the long, dark tunnel she had been going down all this time.

In a small way, Audric had just lightened it a wee bit with his words. Or should she say by sharing Fraser's actions? Not only had she worried endlessly about her kin's safety, but their mental well-being. She knew what it felt like to be the one left behind. How awful the loneliness when all hope faded.

Though Fraser hadn't stayed on with them, he had offered her parents and sisters something she never had when it came to her husband and daughter. Vengeance. They might have had to let her go, but they retained the certain knowledge that Fraser would see her avenged. That he would end her captor's life as ruthlessly as he had supposedly ended hers.

And Fraser would have had she not begged him to stay his hand.

Which showed the sort of man he really was.

What he was capable of. What he had been capable of since this all began.

He had used his wits and wiles, embraced something he despised, and never gave up. And though Audric had not said it in so many words, he also reminded her that at the peak of rage, Fraser didn't lose himself but thought rationally. He did so the night she was taken, and again during this recent sea battle. Then yet again when he didn't end Estienne when he had the chance.

As she had speculated, Fraser was a man who would listen before acting impulsively. He would keep things in perspective. He had proven it time and time again. So was it fair then that she gave up on him now by not putting her full trust in him? Did he not deserve such after all he had done for her?

He did. She knew he did. But that made it no easier to confess. Because once she did, she had no control over what happened.

She might not be able to save his life.

Chapter Eleven

FRASER SAT AT his desk and continued to watch Elspeth sleep. After keeping a discreet eye on her the previous night as she stood outside for hours, he pretended to be asleep when she returned. Though he wanted to confront her and continue their conversation, he decided to wait for her to come to him.

He would not force secrets out of her.

She had been through far too much.

When she dozed off in a chair rather than lie down beside him, he transferred her to the bed. Though tempted to join her and pull her into his arms he instead spent the remainder of the night sitting at his desk staring out to sea.

Now, like a lovesick fool who ought to know better, he gazed at her. It was still hard to believe she was here. That she lived. It felt surreal in an unexplainable way. As if he had yet to awaken from a dream.

He had stood over her several times as she tossed and turned, caught in sleep that seemed as restless as his soul. When she muttered in distress, and her eyelids fluttered, he almost found himself offering comfort. Many times he nearly sat and rested her head on his lap. Many times he longed to caress her soft skin and remind her she was no longer caught in a nightmare.

Yet he did none of those things.

Instead, he eventually set her ring on his desk and joined Magnus above deck. All was as it should be and the weather seemed fair enough.

"As ye ordered we remain just enough off the coast to avoid detection," Magnus reported. "We're through the Firth and dropped our speed." He nodded at Fraser. "Everything's going precisely as ye said it would Cap'n." Then he shook his head. "Yer a smart bastard."

Fraser winked then eyed the crew. "What're the men sayin'?"

Magnus didn't need to ask what he meant. "They like her."

"Do they trust her?"

"Aye."

"And ye?" he asked, already knowing the answer.

While some might dance around an answer to appease him, his first mate was no such man. "Not at all."

"Nor should ye," Fraser replied. "Not yet anyway."

He clasped Magnus' shoulder before he decided to break his fast with those of the crew not seeing to the sail's. Unlike most captains, he spent nearly as much time with the men as his quartermaster. He liked to be in the thick of it and cut out the middle man on occasion. As Magnus had said, they seemed fond of Elspeth. The one whose face was cut wore his bandage like a badge of honor, seemingly her new protector if she found herself in need.

By the time he returned to his cabin with food for her, she was staring out the window with her arms crossed over her chest. She seemed lost in thought. As if mayhap contemplating how she wanted to phrase things. How she wanted to approach him this time. Would they bicker again or was that behind them?

"I see we're already through the Pentland Firth and a ways down the west coast," she finally said, her back still to him. "You're making good time."

"Aye," he replied. "Come eat, Elspeth. Ye barely touched a thing last night."

"The wind's in your favor too," she remarked, making no mention of food.

So she wished to talk then. Good.

"We'll drop anchor for a few hours," he said as he joined her. "Then continue on when the time's right."

She frowned, her mental wheels spinning. "Would it not be better to keep going?"

"We'll be sailing into a storm," he supplied. "'Tis best to travel through it at high tide."

It would be best not to travel it at all, but they would nonetheless.

A fact that made her eyes narrow on him.

"Och," she whispered as she figured things out damn fast. "Pirates are always talking. Ye must have caught rumor of bad weather." She shook her head. "Nay, my guess is ye purposefully asked in port about the weather on this side of Scotland. Ye were scheming." Her eyes narrowed further still. "What are ye up to, Fraser?"

He arched a brow and didn't budge an inch. "What are *ye* up to, Elspeth?"

"Are we back to that then?" she murmured.

"I dinnae think we ever left it."

Their eyes stayed with one another's as she appeared to mull something over. She might be testing his patience, but he enjoyed how the copper in her eyes brightened when she was set to be cunning. It reminded him of the fire that flared in their depths when she was in the heat of passion.

Her eyes remained narrowed as she finally put all the pieces together. "Ye know dinnae ye." Her gaze drifted back to the water. "That's why ye went this way rather than through the southern channel."

"Aye, I know," he replied. "I have all along."

What she referred to was the fact that Estienne was following them at a distance.

Elspeth closed her eyes and shook her head. "Which means ye knew there was another ship waiting to pick him up. Two ships actually." She looked skyward before her eyes returned to him. "Which means ye know why I'm here."

"Aye," he said softly. "What I havenae been able to figure out yet are your intentions." He scowled. "Other than that they arenae in my favor."

"I warned him ye were no fool," she muttered as she braced her hands on the sill and looked to the sea again. "I knew better than to ignore the rumors about ye, but I thought mayhap…"

He tried to ignore how much that stung. How she had undoubtedly tried to betray him.

"Whilst at one time I would have assumed ye spoke of Estienne," he said darkly. "I now know he is but his father's puppet." While tempted to shake some sense into her, he had to remain calm and get to the root of things. "What bargain did ye strike with André? What did he promise ye in exchange for my head?"

In truth, he would have gladly forfeited his life to free her of that monster. Yet as she made so clear yesterday, she knew how to take care of herself regardless of who she had to step on to get there.

"'Twas not your head he was after." She inhaled deeply before turning steady eyes his way. "'Twas what ye possess. What will finally get him his treasure." Her eyes narrowed again. "Where are they, Fraser? Where are my stones?"

So that was the crux of it. The reason for the whole bloody charade with Estienne's ship yesterday. To get her on board, and lead Fraser and his stones straight into a trap. As it was, had they simply lured him to land with any other excuse there was no guarantee he would have had the rocks with him.

Yet he wondered.

"There's more to this." He crossed his arms over his chest. "Tell me what he wants beyond treasure."

"Is treasure not enough?"

"Not always." He stepped a little closer, watching her intently. She might be putting up a good front, but he saw telltale signs of more deception. A tiny vein in her neck throbbing. The tight line of her lips. She was hiding something. "Tell me, lass. Save me from sailing my men into certain death."

"Save ye," she whispered as her eyes caught his. "That's all I've been trying to do."

She sighed and shook her head. Her voice wobbled some, but she kept going.

"Though the son wanted a pet, 'twas always his father that wanted more," she explained, her eyes troubled. "Ye havenae heard of André because he wasnae a pirate originally but defected from *La Royale* to enjoy darker pursuits. To gain more wealth than what his country could offer." She visibly shivered. "To satisfy the sinister longings he was forced to keep repressed."

So he was once part of the French navy. Not overly surprising really. Sailors did such on occasion. Typically, they leaned toward privateering first, but it sounded like André was by far a different sort of creature entirely.

It also sounded like Elspeth was finally ready to be honest.

"Whilst he was certainly indulging Estienne by letting him keep me," anger flashed in her eyes, "'twas also a way to keep me under his thumb, in a prison of sorts, as he readied his crew and established a stronghold. Which, naturally, needs financing."

"Where is this stronghold?"

"Verra close to where my clan was originally from," she replied.

"'Tis his hope to eventually ally himself with either the *Devils of the Deep* or mayhap *Poseidon's Legion*."

"Och," he muttered. "He'll not have the chance."

"Let's hope not," she murmured.

"'Tis hard to believe he let ye out of his sight to sail with Estienne." His eyes never left her face. "'Tis equally hard to imagine that he had time to whip ye but not rape ye."

"His ways were a bit more sadistic and twisted than that," she said softly, her jaw set as she clearly fought bad memories. "Though I'm sure that might change in the future."

"Bloody hell," he said through clenched teeth as he understood her meaning. He knew of men who found more pleasure in watching the beating of a lass than the baser act of laying with her.

Betrayal or not, he couldn't help but reel her close and rest her cheek against his chest. How many times had she been beaten for André's benefit? Her soft skin wounded to give him pleasure? Unimaginable rage filled him as he thought about it. As he realized the hell she must have been living in even before she ended up on Estienne's ship.

"It wasnae just my kin's life he said he would spare if I brought him the stones," she whispered, "but yours, Fraser."

"And ye actually thought he would keep his word?" He cupped the back of her neck beneath her hair as he had once done. "Ye *cannae* be that naïve, lass."

"'Twas not just now that I bargained for your life." She pulled back and met his eyes. "But all along."

When her hand rested on his chest, he realized she wore his ring again.

"The only reason Estienne has kept ye in his tailwind and not had ye slain in your sleep all this time is because I've promised myself to André." Her lower lip trembled slightly before she bit down on it. "And I promised him when he was ready, I would find a way to lead ye back to MacLauchlin land with the stones." She shook her head, her eyes moist as they searched his. "Dinnae ye ken yet? This ruse was *my* idea, Fraser."

"And 'twas a bloody good one," he assured, grateful for her cleverness. It didn't matter who came up with the plan because he was making it work in his favor. Honestly, he was surprised André hadn't done it sooner. But then he understood the logic in a defector maintaining anonymity until he was in a good position to defend himself.

"Surely ye suspected someone would be coming after you eventually when ye took those stones," she said. "Ye must have been prepared for it."

"Aye, I knew the day would come," he replied. "I would have sold my soul for it to come sooner and my enemy within arm's reach." His gaze stayed with hers. "Now the day has come. *Ye* have come." His eyes flickered from the ring back to her face. "And ye wearing that now tells me ye have decided not to go it alone…ye've decided to trust me."

"Aye," she whispered. "And 'tis no greater trust to be given than allowing ye to protect the man I love…the man I've *always* loved."

No words had ever sounded better.

"Did ye not think I could defend myself, lass?"

"Not as well as I could have defended ye," she assured, cocky. "As I have all along." She peered at him, concerned as she revealed what had really been at the root of her deception. "Now ye know the truth I fear ye will think with your heart rather than your mind. And when ye do, he will use that." She shook her head "He will use me against ye somehow, Fraser."

He offered a slow grin. "Not if I use someone else against him first."

Her eyes lingered on his for a moment before understanding dawned, and her gaze flickered from the ocean back to him. "Estienne."

"Aye." He took the hand that had been resting on his chest and began dropping small kisses on each knuckle. "He'll be captured by nightfall."

"Sounds devious," she murmured, her eyelids half-mast as he massaged the back of her neck and ran the pad of his thumb along her sensitive jawline.

"Oh, 'tis devious," he assured, grateful to have her in his arms again. To see the pleasure in her eyes.

"I'm sorry," she whispered. "About trying to deceive ye no matter my good intentions…for not listening that night two winters ago…"

He knew she hadn't listened. That she had feared for her kin's safety and not stayed behind the rock. And while he was angry at first, he did not hold it against her overly long. He understood how much she loved her family and knew full well he would have done the same for his own.

"'Tis all behind us now, lass," he whispered before he brushed his lips across hers then tilted her chin until her eyes stayed with his. "There will be no more lying, though, aye? Ye willnae battle me anymore but allow me to fight alongside ye?"

A small smile curled her lips. "'Tis a lot to promise." Her smile widened. "Though I see ye have the right of how things should be betwixt us when it comes to battling."

He knew she would appreciate that. And truth be told he liked it immensely. He liked that she could battle with the best of them and hold her own. Not only that but she seemed to enjoy it as much as him. It had never been that way with other lasses. The last lass. If anything, she found his passion for fighting troubling at times. It had been a point of contention.

Interesting, in retrospect, how destiny worked.

Because he knew very well it had played a part in bringing him together with Elspeth. He knew without hesitation that it had resurrected something he thought lost to him in more ways than one.

"You're an admirable ally, lass," he murmured, more than willing to pay her the compliment she deserved as he brushed another kiss across her lips. "'Twould be foolish of me to think otherwise."

"As ye learned on the enemy's ship yesterday," she agreed.

"As I *almost* learned," he countered, grinning.

It had been a long time since his smile was genuine. He had missed the feeling. Her. This. And showed her as much with a considerably longer kiss. One that found her perched on the opposite side of his desk this time.

Long overdue, desperate to *see* her, be *inside* her, he pulled her shirt over her head and finally feasted his eyes on her nudity. As he always knew she would be, she was perfectly made with delicate bones, satiny smooth skin, lush breasts, and a tight wee waist.

She gave him little time to admire her as she pulled his lips back to hers. The kiss she gave him this time was far more insistent as was the way she pressed her hot center against him. He had never wanted anyone as much as he wanted her right now. Eager, impatient, both breathed heavily as he began to tug her trousers off.

The moment was nearly here.

A moment he never thought would come.

"Cap'n!" came a much unwanted voice. "Ye said to let ye know when we were close."

"Aye, Magnus," he roared. He swore his first mate did this on purpose. "And you've let me know!"

"Aye, Cap'n," Magnus agreed as Fraser twirled his tongue around one pert, delicious nipple, enjoying her groan as he prayed his first mate would go away.

"I think mayhap ye'll want to reassess the situation," Magnus continued, dashing his hopes. "The fog's comin' in earlier than expected."

"'Tis good that," he growled before he returned to her lips and wrapped his tongue with hers.

"As is the storm," Magnus added.

"Bloody hell," he growled as he reluctantly tore his lips from hers. He cursed a few more times and hung his head. That unfortunately put a swift end to things.

After all, the storm was an integral part of his plan.

Chapter Twelve

ELSPETH STOOD ON the helm next to Fraser, impressed by his plan. "Ye got lucky with this weather, aye?" Eyes narrowed on the heavy fog bank they were heading into, she sought out the others, but there was no sign of them. "Douglas' and Innis' ships are well and truly hidden."

Because of the time of year, cold and warm fronts came together more often in this area, and Fraser intended to use that to his advantage. Not only would Estienne's two ships be blinded by fog, allowing *The Sea Hellions* to position themselves favorably, but he was being led straight into dangerous waters.

"'Twould have been better if the weather held off a bit longer," Fraser commented, eying his sails before he shrugged, fearless. "But 'twill not be the first time we've had to ride out a storm the likes of this one."

The sails were being reefed just enough to allow for maneuverability.

As was pre-planned, when Fraser ordered his men to grab what they could off Estienne's ships, it wasn't for what meager loot they could gather but to provide weight on *The Sea Hellions*' ships. Now all three hulls were made heavier with evenly distributed, strapped down weight. As it were, speed would soon become less important than keeping the ships from flipping.

He eyed her curiously. "Are ye ready for this, lass?"

"Och, aye!" she exclaimed, grinning. If anything had offered her pleasure through the endless darkness over the past few years, it was the thrill of being on the sea during a good storm.

Fraser chuckled and shook his head. "Mayhap ye've gone a wee bit mad after all?"

"No madder than ye," she pointed out, well aware his excitement didn't entirely have to do with finally getting his hands on the enemy.

"You'll take shelter in my cabin when it gets bad," he assumed.

She shook her head. "I'll do no such thing."

About to remark that he should know her better than that by now, she snapped her mouth shut when he handed her a leather strap with a twinkle in his eyes. "Then ye will at least strap down, aye?"

He had known all along she intended to remain on deck.

"Aye, Cap'n," she assured, her smile as rakish as his as they anticipated what lay on the horizon. A raging storm, death to their enemies and soon enough, a welcome reunion with her kin. She set aside all thought that André might be with them right now. That he might have hurt them.

"'Twill speak of how well ye all work together if ye pull this off," she murmured, eager to see his plan in action. "And how well ye sail this ship." She gave him the praise he deserved. "If 'tis half as good as what ye displayed yesterday we should be just fine."

"Aye, lass," he replied. "The key will be in stealing Estienne away whilst still in the fog." The corner of his mouth shot up. "Then we'll give his crew a merry chase through the storm."

"So they dinnae have a chance to fire off a cannon, aye?"

"Aye." He shook his head. "If they do I can only hope the severity of the storm will mask the sound."

Though they were a ways from shore, she understood his concern. Sound could carry on the wind, and they didn't want André to be alarmed. As far as he knew, Fraser would be sailing into harbor ignorant of Estienne's presence.

"I hope Innis takes care," she said softly as the fog kept thickening. "And remains out of the line of fire."

As it stood, Innis should at this moment be sneaking up on Estienne's ship, set to kidnap the captain out from under his crew's noses. Once they had him, they would let Estienne's men know, and the pursuit would begin.

"Dinnae worry about Innis. He's a bloody good captain," Fraser said. "Not to mention, he has a man that can sneak up on a ship undetected and snatch just about anything. Especially in this kind of fog."

She nodded, understanding why Innis' ship was the best choice to keep Estienne on right now. Of the three men, he was the least likely to end the enemy before they put him to good use.

Time seemed to crawl as they waited.

The sea was eerily calm, but it could get that way sometimes before gales swept through. Fraser's crew was impressive as they worked silently, manning the ship with smooth efficiency. It was clear that they were a seasoned group of sailors and worked well together.

Regrettably, that was not always the case on a pirate ship. She had seen her fair share of men challenge Estienne for his position only to die beneath his blade. As a rule, mayhem was more constant than not in his circles.

Fraser, however, didn't appear to have that sort of dissent on his ship. The minor uproar yesterday, of course, was to be expected and had been dealt with. Well, somewhat. The conundrum of whether or not they would find treasure to provide them with was a lingering concern.

One thing at a time though.

First, they needed to capture Estienne.

The minutes continued to tick by slowly as they waited. Rare was the man who could sneak onto a pirate ship and kidnap their captain without his crew being the wiser. Yet Fraser seemed confident, so she had to trust in that.

"Cap'n," Magnus whispered, gesturing off the starboard side.

"Och, just look at that," she whispered, unable to contain an impressed grin as a man in a skiff rowed by. With a wad of material stuffed in his mouth and his hands tied behind his back, none other than Estienne sat across from him. When his eyes narrowed up at her, she kept grinning and winked.

He was in for it now.

Fraser made a silent signal to his men to pick up speed. His ship was built for battle and Innis' and Douglas' for speed, so it was best that he gained momentum now and let them catch up.

Soon after that, the water grew choppy, and rain began to spit. Thunder rumbled, and lightning flashed through the fog ahead. Well aware of how storms could act, Elspeth strapped off, ready to ride it out.

If this went as planned, there would be little if any battling.

At least not with men.

Winds began to gust, and swollen sails lurched them forward as Fraser took to the wheel. What he was about to do was borderline suicidal, but he seemed unfazed by the danger ahead. Rather, zealous confidence lit his eyes as he steered into the waves.

Moments later, the fog began to clear only to be replaced with heavier rain and darker seas. It wasn't long before they saw what they wanted to see. Estienne's ships had done precisely what Fraser hoped and pursued Innis once they realized he had stolen their captain.

Estienne might not be any great treasure but sailing into a raging storm to save him beat facing André's wrath if they didn't get him back.

Innis was in the front, the two enemy ships in his wake and Douglas followed from behind. Trapped, they now had Fraser on their right and the shore on their left. But the shore would not be their ultimate fate. That might warn André trouble was afoot.

Best that none lived that long. After all, dead men told no tales.

Waves grew taller, and sea spray pounded them from every direction. His legs braced and his muscles straining, Fraser held tight to the wheel and steered steadily. The hull creaked and groaned as the ship rocked back and forth. Yet he kept cutting it through the water at an admirable pace considering its bulk.

What it lacked in speed, *The Sea Rogue* more than made up for in intimidation.

It might be storming and the seas rough, but there was still enough visibility for the enemy to see an imposing ship with its broadside guns aimed their way. That meant while they were fighting this storm, they were also preparing for battle.

Or so Fraser and his crew hoped.

Because if the enemy were doing what any crew in their right mind should be at the moment, they would be paying less attention to what lay ahead. A death some might say more terrifying than a firestorm of cannons.

"*Coire Bhreacain,*" she whispered, peering ahead. Often referred to as the cauldron of the speckled seas the Gulf of Corryvreckan not only possessed dangerous tides but a far greater threat.

A whirlpool.

Wave by dooming wave, they grew closer to an especially perilous area, made far worse in this weather. Winds gusted, and the ships lurched, but they plowed on. It would all come down to perfect timing and the grace of God himself. If this wasn't done with exact precision,

The Sea Hellions could very well suffer the same fate as their enemies.

Chuckling all the while, relish lit Fraser's eyes as he kept on course, passing between the isles of Scarba and Jura as they approached the whirlpool. She shook her head and met his grin. And he called *her* mad. But she didn't blame him. This was excitement at its best.

The closer they got the louder the roar of Corryvreckan.

Her heart pounded wildly as they crested a wave and raced in its direction. Nothing matched the sight of such a beast during a violent storm. White and frothing, it bared its rabid and ravenous teeth against the blackened angry sky. It was every man's worst nightmare. A ferocious jaw of swirling damnation.

"Aye then laddies 'tis time," Fraser muttered as he white-knuckled the wheel, put more weight into it and cranked it just enough.

His words were for Innis and Douglas whose ships were doing the same. Just in the nick of time too. Or was it? Because at first *The Sea Rogue* dragged, caught in the far outer currents of the whirlpool. The sails whipped and dragged, fighting Fraser.

Yet he fought right back, laughing the whole time.

She had never seen anything like it. Where his men should be terrified, they seemed relatively calm, many chuckling alongside their captain as they unfurled the sails completely. They had *that* much faith in Fraser. So did she for that matter. Unable to help herself, free in a way she had never been before, she tossed her head back and laughed.

Now, *this* was living.

Luckily, or quite expectedly considering Fraser's easy manner, a hearty gust steered them free just in time. Though for a frightening moment it looked like the others might be lost to them, Innis' ship finally broke free as did her brother's.

Just as they had hoped, the enemy ships had no such luck.

"Ballocks, just look at that," she whispered, wide-eyed as the enemy crews lost all control over the ships and they began listing and bobbing precariously. Between the sound of the storm and the whirlpool itself, the terrified roars of men were drowned out as many abandoned ship.

But it was too late.

There was no hope of escape.

The ships began cracking as the heart of the maelstrom ravaged its prey. Masts snapped, and sails ripped as one ship flipped. Soon, still caught in a relentless, hungry clockwise current, its bow dove and its stern flipped up in the air.

Moments later the other ship, still afloat, rushed past only for the stern of the capsizing ship to snap and slam down on it. A chaotic cluster of jumbled wood, twisted sails, and broken bodies were soon fully consumed as the Corryvreckan welcomed a small army of souls to the ocean floor.

Though the seas were still rough, the storm dwindled down substantially as they made their way free of the straightaway and into the sound off Argyll. They had done it. Fraser and his fleet had *all* done it.

And they had done so without losing Estienne.

Now *The Sea Hellions* would stay adrift just offshore and apart from one another, so they didn't draw unwanted attention. They would wait and watch until they made their next move. One she suspected would prove far more perilous than what they had just faced.

"Come, lass," Fraser murmured, untying her strap. "Let's get ye warmed up."

She had been so caught up in the rush of what just happened she didn't realize she was shivering. Nor did she particularly care.

"Och, I'm warm enough," she said absently. Her heart still raced as she wiped a sodden lock of hair out of her eyes with a shaky hand. "'Tis just excitement from the ride."

"Ye arenae nearly warm enough," he murmured. His voice deepened as his hand lingered on her hip. "Nor am I."

Her heart began racing for another reason entirely as she met his eyes.

Drowned in them.

Once again, they were in that cave in Stonehaven. The promise in his gaze just as intense now as it had been then. Only now there was the added wait. The endless years, weeks, days and even hours that had stood between them finally coming together.

But no more.

"Aye, Cap'n," she whispered. "I think 'tis high past time ye warmed me up."

That's all she got out before he swept her off her feet and the thrill of the ride she had just experienced paled in comparison to what was soon to come.

Chapter Thirteen

H E HAD WAITED over two long winters for this moment but had no choice but to wait a few minutes longer. Everyone had been ordered, including the other captains, to keep a vigilant eye to the sea for a while after the enemy's ships had been sunk. They needed to be sure André and his men had not seen anything.

Fraser and *The Sea Hellions* would head for shore in the pre-dawn hours of the following morn when the enemy rested. Then they would strike.

"Ye remain confident that André would attack now if he saw anything, aye?" he asked Elspeth as he kicked the door shut behind them and set her down.

"Aye." She nodded. "He would not lie in wait if he thought his son was in harm's way."

"Good." He handed her a mug of whisky, and a blanket then pulled some dried meats and cheese out of a satchel he had grabbed on the way. "Time for ye to have some food and drink, as well as get those wet clothes off."

"In which order," she said softly as she stepped closer. As it was for him, her lust for the storm had swiftly turned to another kind of lust altogether. "Because I'm not so sure we'll do much eating or drinking once—"

He put a finger to her lips and silenced her. "Clothes first, then food and drink then…" His eyes trailed down her hungrily. "Then far more."

They might need to keep an eye out for a bit, but nothing said the time could not be passed pleasurably enough. She made that painfully evident when she proceeded to take her time undressing, her eyes never leaving his.

"Now that we have some time alone," she murmured as she peeled off her wet shirt and revealed glistening breasts and tight pink nipples. "Why dinnae ye share with me what ye remember about yourself."

"Aye," he managed, his voice hoarse from arousal as he watched her while pulling off his own sopping tunic. "'Twas…more than I could have imagined."

"Aye?" Her eyes piqued with curiosity as she yanked off one boot. "How so?"

He had long thought about how he wanted to present what he had learned. The remarkable and fantastical truths. Yet now that the moment had arrived, he wasn't quite sure how to go about it.

"Fraser?" Her brows furrowed in concern as she removed her other boot. "Are ye all right?"

"Aye." He nodded as he tore his eyes from her and gazed outside while he took off his boots as well. Mayhap if he didn't look at her, it would come easier. "Do ye recall what we talked about in regards to my clan?"

"Aye." She wiggled out of her trousers. "That they were powerful."

"They are," he agreed. Though he tried like hell to keep his eyes off her, he just couldn't help himself. Even with her back turned to him, she was too alluring with her wee firm arse and shapely legs.

"Fraser," she murmured, eying him over her shoulder.

He blinked and dragged his eyes to her face. "Aye?"

"What else did ye learn besides what we already discussed?"

Right. That. "Blanket first."

When she cocked her head in confusion, he gestured at the blanket. "Wrap yourself, so I can think clearly enough to speak, aye?"

She smiled and nodded, wrapping it around her before she took a sip of whisky.

"As it turns out," he continued, removing his drenched breeches. "The rumors of Clan MacLomain are indeed verra much true."

"What's not true?" she whispered, not sounding like herself. As it turned out, she was in the same stupefied state he had just suffered. Slack-jawed, her avid eyes were lustful as she gazed at his nudity.

"Nay, the rumors of my kin *are* true," he corrected, grinning.

Though tempted to keep her ensorcelled until he had his way with her, they needed to remain focused. So he wrapped a blanket around himself and urged her to sit and eat as he kept an eye to the sea. "The stories shared around campfires about my clan are verra much based on fact, lass."

She nibbled on cheese and eyed him with a smirk. "Ye mean about wizards and witches and such?"

"Aye." He sat beside her, facing the water. "'Tis truly a mystical clan, Elspeth."

He explained things the best he could to someone who only thought stories such as his were fairytales. But all fairytales had some grain of truth and Scotland was richer than most when it came to folklore. While tempted to go into more detail, for now, he chose to remain vague. She would learn soon enough.

"Someday soon we will visit my home," he assured, "and ye will meet my kin."

"I would verra much like that," she said softly. "So 'tis a clan that practices the old ways?" He was pleased she seemed to believe him where most would not. "'Tis as Innis speculated then? You're of druid blood?"

He supposed that was one way to look at it.

"In a way, aye…but more so." Fraser shook his head. "In my case 'tis verra good intuition or foresight, I suppose."

Her brows shot up. "It almost sounds like witchcraft." She shrugged, not all that put off by it or perhaps not really believing it. Pirates especially were known for embellishing and telling a good tall tale. "Though 'twould come in handy through all this."

"Aye," he agreed. "If only I could pick and choose when it happened." He shook his head. "But that is neither here nor there and not relevant to this…us." He took her hand. "I would rather speak of the day we first met."

"The day ye nearly died," she murmured with a frown.

"Aye." Again, he was careful with his words. "As ye gathered I had been battling and was nearly defeated. Where that was or who I fought no longer matters. What *does* matter is the lass I left behind…more so *how* I left her behind."

Something indefinable flashed in her eyes as she whispered, "So there *is* another lass?"

"Not anymore," he said softly, still recalling the day he rode away from her. "Her name was Kenna…Kenna MacLauchlin. And she has since died in battle."

"I'm so sorry," she began before her brows snapped together. "MacLauchlin, aye?"

"Aye, mayhap a distant relation," he murmured. "But that isnae the point." He glanced out the window again to make sure all was well before he continued. "The point is I let the love betwixt us slip away because I didnae recognize it for what it was. How powerful and important it had been." He cupped her cheek. "'Tis the verra same thing I've seen in ye from nearly the moment our eyes met." He shook his head. "And I willnae let it go this time. I willnae be so foolish."

"Why does it almost sound like you're apologizing to me?" she whispered. "In hopes that she hears it?"

Because in some ways it was very much that. Or so he had speculated from the moment he remembered his past. The moment he recalled Kenna and realized how eerily similar she was to Elspeth. And when one knew that love could, in fact, transcend time and even that reincarnation existed, one paid attention to such things.

"'Tis just that ye remind me of her is all," he said softly. "Our clans were allied, so we grew up together. She had the same fierce free spirit and the same light in her eyes when she laughed. The same passion and love for her people and country."

"She sounds admirable," she murmured. "Someone I would have liked."

"Aye." His hand drifted to the side of her neck. "As she would have liked ye…verra much."

"'Tis good to hear." Her eyes held his. "And 'tis also good to know ye feel so strongly about me…" A knowing smile curled her lips. "Though I didnae doubt it."

"Good," he replied. "But it needed to be said regardless."

Because he would not make the same mistake twice.

"Aye then." She brushed her lips across his and whispered, "How long do we need to keep an eye on the sea, Cap'n?"

"Not that much longer," he assured, just as eager. He gestured at the food. "Eat, lass."

Though he would much prefer remaining by her side, he stood in front of the windows before she ended up on his desk again. Yet it seemed she would not let him get away that easy.

Food in hand, she joined him. "There is one thing I havenae figured out yet."

He knew what she was going to say because the same thing had been weighing on his mind. "What if there isnae treasure?" He perked a brow at her. "What if ye have convinced my crew to fight for something that doesnae exist?"

"Aye." She slanted a look at him. "I've heard it told that you're verra clever. Have ye any grand ideas?"

"Not yet," he replied. "Though I've given your parents and people coin when I can, I've only a small stash to get them out of there if need be." He shook his head. "'Twill not be enough to satisfy three crews." Yet he speculated. "But then ye never know what could turn up in André's camp."

"True." She grinned, catching on. Not only would André have the bulk of his wealth there but who knew what else a defector of the French navy might be carrying.

"Where are the stones?" she murmured as she polished off her cheese.

He crouched, unlocked a secret compartment in his desk and handed them over.

"Ballocks." Fists planted on her hips, she cocked her head and narrowed her eyes at the secret slot. "I snooped all around there!"

Of course, she had. What sort of pirate would she be otherwise?

"'Twould have done ye no good without a key," he reminded.

She snorted and shot him an exasperated look. "Do ye think I dinnae know how to pick a lock by now?"

"I would hope." He grinned and shrugged. "I guess your pirate cunning was lacking this time then." He considered her. "Or mayhap ye didnae *truly* want to find them just yet." He stepped closer. "Mayhap deep down ye wanted to keep me by your side till the end."

"Mayhap," she whispered as her promising eyes rose to his. "Till the end to be sure."

It took all he had not to kiss her then. Not to make her his. But they still had things to discuss. Like the treasure. So he gestured at the stones. "If ye couldnae find the castle ruins before what makes ye think we will be able to now?"

"I dinnae know," she murmured. "Hope I suppose. A clearer mind than what I suffered when I was there last. 'Twas not easy to see straight when I thought my daughter's life at risk." Her eyes went to the stones again. "And mayhap with these along things will be more obvious than they were before."

"How so?"

"The rocks come from the remnants of MacLauchlin Castle." She shrugged. "So mayhap something will stand out that didnae before. Mayhap the stones will match something in the landscape. Namely the castle itself."

He sighed. "'Tis a lot to hope for."

"Aye, but hope we must." She looked at the sky. "We'll need the clouds to clear as well. We'll need help from the stars."

"Ah, I often wondered if the marks on the stones didnae have to do with the constellations," he remarked. "Though when I pieced them together, I couldnae seem to make sense of it."

"'Tis not constellations we're looking for but one star." Elspeth laid the stones on his desk and began moving them around until they fit together well enough. She pointed at the circular mark at the top. "If we line these up with the brightest star in the northern sky when standing on the castle ruins, all the marks beneath it will point the way. They signify landmarks of some sort."

"Landmarks." Not reassuring. "That could be a wee bit tricky."

"Aye." Her worried eyes returned to his as she shared his concern. "Because now we have no choice but to hope they're still there after a century." She shook her head. "Otherwise, the treasure is lost to us forever."

Chapter Fourteen

Elspeth could tell by the doubtful look in Fraser's eyes that he wasn't holding out much hope of finding the treasure. Not only was it likely the land had changed, but countless others had been there searching before them and never found it.

"It cannae hurt to look," she said softly.

"Aye, lass," he agreed, shifting closer as she fiddled with the stones. She had tried to ignore these things her whole life. The sadness that lay at the heart of them. The wayward path they had led her family down.

Yet here she was following that path regardless.

On a journey she never could have anticipated.

"So ye stand in a certain spot," he murmured, trailing his fingers over hers. "Then ye find your treasure."

She knew precisely what treasure he was talking about now and it had nothing to do with the stones. Her eyes drifted to him as the hard, well-defined muscles of his chest and abdomen peeked out from behind the blanket.

"I think mayhap I'd rather go searching for treasure sooner rather than later," he murmured, his voice softer still as he brushed his fingers down her neck and over her collarbone.

"Are we not keeping watch for the enemy anymore?" she managed, her throat suddenly dry. Breathing became more difficult as he pulled her hand away from where she held her blanket together.

"I think it has been long enough," he replied, his voice deepening with arousal. "And many eyes remain where they should."

"But not yours," she whispered as his fingers continued to wander. When they trailed between her breasts, she shivered with awareness. Gooseflesh raced along her torso and limbs as he lightly dusted the underside of one breast before fully removing her blanket.

"Nay, my eyes are right where they should be," he murmured as he stepped behind her and began to gently kiss along her scars. He spent ample time there as though trying to take away pain that no longer existed. In fact, his touch was so tender and caring it brought tears to her eyes.

When he, at last, turned her back, his blanket was gone.

"Fraser…" was all she could manage, the word a hoarse whisper when he pulled her against him. She had never been so aroused. So aware of the feel of another's flesh against hers. The marked difference between them.

His hard body against her softness.

His steely length pulsing and ready for her.

Ravenous, ready, she welcomed his kiss…his urgency.

When he hoisted her up, she wrapped her arms and legs around him, certain they would end up on his desk again. Instead, he kneaded her backside and continued kissing her as he walked her to the bed. Impassioned, never wanting to let go, she tangled her hands in his hair as he climbed onto the bed and rested her against the headboard.

Nailed to the wall, it was shaped like the curve of a ship and at the perfect height to support her. When his lips left hers and began trailing down her neck, she tightened her legs and groaned, sending a very clear message.

She wanted him now.

No more waiting.

When his eyes returned to hers, the predatory sensual heat gathered in their blue depths was unmistakable. He appreciated that she knew what she wanted and demanded that he give it to her now. She was no chaste, innocent girl but a woman eager to see what pleasures he could bring.

Would it be all that she had imagined? Would this driving ache that haunted her when she thought of him finally be assuaged? Could it possibly be? Or had she built him up in her mind to such a degree that he could not possibly satisfy the high bar she had set?

Almost as if he followed her thoughts, he offered a small, cocksure turn of his lips before he clasped her backside with one strong hand, the headboard with the other and thrust deep.

She didn't just moan but cried out in shameless pleasure.

The sway of the ship didn't throw him off balance at all as he thrust even deeper, daring her to embrace everything he offered. A slew of inescapable sensations. Wicked desire. Near painful passion.

Yet he controlled what he gave her.

What he allowed.

Desperate, she writhed against him, but he purposefully kept what she needed just out of reach as his eyes stayed with hers. Yet she saw the unfiltered truth. The burning need in his darkened gaze.

Holding back was no longer possible.

Teasing and drawing out the moment was no longer an option.

His tether on control had snapped.

Now a sensual storm of wicked pleasure built. A raging swell of yearning. A tsunami of frenzied lust they would gladly drown in if it meant finding what had long eluded them.

His brows lowered sharply in concentration as he increased his pace. She bit her lower lip, dug her nails into his sides and watched him from beneath heavy lids. His sweat slicked body. The mesmerizing flex of his muscles. Seeing him like this only added to everything she felt.

It intensified the friction and magnificent pressure building at her core.

Like him, she was desperate to dive off the tall peak they were climbing. Greedy to crest wherever they were going. Breathing heavily, her heart pounding in her throat, she met his thrusts, grunts, and groans.

They were animalistic, lost in instinct, gone in near violent ardor.

At some point, she wrapped her arms around his broad shoulders and dug her nails in deep. She held on for dear life, afraid to let go.

"Elspeth," he moaned through clenched teeth.

It was that, the near worshiping, desperate way he said her name, that made her come undone. She dug her nails in deeper still, flung her head back, and released a roar to rival the thunder rumbling across the sky. Pressing deep, he growled, locked up then released a ragged groan of profound satisfaction.

What they just shared was undeniable.

Potent. Life changing.

Forever.

Hearts pounding, breath ragged, they stayed that way, languishing in residual pleasure. By the time he finally pulled her down to the bed, she could barely keep her eyes open. She was only vaguely aware of him tucking her against his side and covering her with a blanket.

"Sleep, lass," he whispered before he kissed her temple. "And dream of treasure."

"I dinnae need to dream," she whispered as she dozed. "I've already found it."

Though she had not meant to say it and tempt Fate, she couldn't help it.

He meant that much.

While he had been vague about his kin, something about his explanation seemed all right...even plausible. She had known from the beginning he was different. Stronger. Healthier. Even nobler. So coming from a clan ripe with actual mysticism was not that far-fetched. Fraser being something more would not surprise her in the least.

But then he was already something more, wasn't he?

He was the man she loved and intended to spend the rest of her life with.

When she awoke again, it was dark, and the seas had calmed considerably. Based on how Fraser stirred when she nuzzled closer, he had been sleeping lightly.

"'Twill all be over soon," he whispered as he kissed the top of her head. "This will all be behind us."

"Aye," she whispered back, twirling the ring on her finger. "Then 'twill be time to look ahead."

"Aye," he murmured.

Eager to make herself clear, she straddled him, and whispered in his ear, "The answer to your question is aye...the answer has *always* been aye."

She didn't need to elaborate. He knew she just said yes to his proposal.

"'Tis bloody good to finally hear though," he growled before he cupped her cheeks and pulled her lips to his.

This time when they made love, it was slow and passionate and lasted the remainder of the night. She lost count of how many times he brought her pleasure. How many times she found release.

Dawn was still a few hours off when they finally left the bed and began getting ready.

"I wish ye would reconsider coming," he muttered as he wrapped his plaid. "Ye could just as easily stay on the ship until 'tis over."

"I'll do no such thing, and ye know better than to wish it," she returned, holding up her wet trousers in dismay. "I'll not miss seeing André and Estienne's end."

"Aye." He sighed, not pressing the issue as he took her trousers and tossed them aside. "Ye cannae wear those."

"Then what," she began, trailing off when he handed her a pair of his breeches and a tunic. "Ye cannae be serious. These are far too large for me."

"Nothing that cannae be adjusted," he assured, urging her to put them on.

By the time he was done dressing her, there was an amused curl to his lips. "Ye look rather becoming actually."

"*Becoming*?" She eyed her outfit dubiously. "More like foolish I'd say."

He had rolled up and tied off the bottom of the pant legs then cinched the material that could have spanned her waist twice with a bandana. His short sleeved tunic went to her elbows, and the front was tied into a knot. His mild amusement spread into a wide smile as he tucked her hair behind her ears and tied yet another bandana around her head.

"There," he declared, nodding with approval. "Ye should be able to move around just fine in that." His wide smile turned into a crooked grin. "A proper pirate lassie if ever I saw one."

"Pirate lassie," she mouthed and shook her head. The truth of it was the outfit *did* allow for good mobility. She eyed him as she strapped on her weapons. "Your scouts should be back by now, aye?"

"Aye," he said. "And if things werenae as they should be there would have already been a knock at my door."

She nodded, wondering what awaited them on shore. André had never allowed Estienne to bring her to this location once he actually settled here. In retrospect, it was wise of him. The less she knew, the better. Point in fact, the ambush she was part of now. Had she known the layout of his developing stronghold, it would have only aided them.

They were about to head up, but Fraser caught her before she got to the door and pulled her close. When he kissed her, it was passionately. All consuming. The sort of kiss that might just land them back in bed.

"Be careful, lass," he murmured as he reluctantly pulled his lips away and brushed his finger along her cheek. "And fight well."

She got the sense as his eyes lingered on hers that he wanted to say more but decided against it. Yet she knew what it was. She could see the love in his eyes. But like her, he knew better than to say it out loud right now. He knew better than to get emotional when they needed to be more focused than ever.

By the time they made it on deck, the ship had moved closer to shore, and the crew had begun making their way toward land.

"André's lookouts have been taken care of," Magnus reported as he joined them. "As we figured, he's been setting up his stronghold verra close to the lass's kin."

Bastard. She would see him dead before he hurt them.

"Aye then," Fraser replied to Magnus before the three of them climbed a ladder down into a skiff. They rode with several others including Audric and Fraser's man-pet Broddy. Audric's eyes flickered knowingly between her and Fraser before he smiled and nodded at her. It seemed he was glad they had finally resolved their issues.

She nodded in return before she looked toward shore. The seas were still choppy but fair enough that an expedition like this wouldn't be too difficult. Thanks to Broddy, Fraser had a good idea where André might have positioned his tent within the encampment.

Nearly everyone was ashore and in position by the time they arrived and snuck into the woods to join Innis and Douglas.

"My swindling devious cutthroat wee lassie," Innis whispered, beaming as he pulled her into his arms and finally greeted her. "'Tis so bloody good to see ye again."

"Aye, my old friend," she whispered. "Ye too."

He kept smiling as he looked her over then nodded with approval. It seemed he liked her new look. She rolled her eyes and gestured at Fraser in explanation as she crouched alongside him.

Estienne was currently leaning against a tree with Douglas' blade to his neck.

"I'm sure your da will be glad to see ye, Estienne," she whispered and offered a wicked grin. "Right before he dies that is."

When his eyes narrowed, she kept a grin firmly in place and was sure to look unaffected. His days of having any sort of control over her were long gone.

"Signal the men." Fraser looked to Innis and Douglas as he unsheathed his sword. "'Tis time."

Blade in hand, she nodded she was ready when Fraser's eyes met hers. She was eager to fight and finally free her village from this ongoing threat. He nodded as though he agreed with her unspoken vow before they made their move.

For all appearances, things went very well as Fraser's men began sneaking into tents and slitting throats before any could call out. She kept her eyes keen as she snuck along, looking for any sign of André. According to Broddy, he was too smart to put himself in an obvious spot. His tent would look like all the others.

As expected, it wasn't long before someone called out that they were under attack, and people started scrambling. The pre-dawn light made it easier to see as she fought and kept searching for the enemy. Taking advantage of her slight size and how rivals underestimated her, she cut down two in a row.

Soon after, she tripped a third man before he got Magnus from behind. Fraser's first mate spun and nodded his thanks before he finished off his opponent.

Her fourth combatant was a bit more of a challenge. He was quick like her, and they circled a few times before she finally got her blade past his defenses and sliced his calf. When he roared in pain and fell to a knee, she ended him then froze.

André had just ducked out of the tent ahead and locked eyes on her.

"To the village," he roared to his men. "Kill them all!"

"I dinnae think so," Fraser called out as he appeared with a blade tight against Estienne's neck. "Not unless ye want me to cut your son's throat."

Nothing was so glorious as seeing the shock on André's face.

The absolute horror.

Yet she should have known things were going too well. That he would have some sort of trick up his sleeve.

"Nay," she whispered, equally horror-stricken as someone tried to dash out of his tent.

"Very good. *Très bon.*" He grabbed her hair and yanked her back against him, meeting Fraser's eyes as his blade met her neck. "Now then, Captain MacLomain. If you let Estienne go, I might just consider letting little Greer go."

Chapter Fifteen

F RASER AND ANDRE'S eyes remained locked as he tried to figure a way out of this. The man was as greasy as his son and easily twice as evil.

Estienne wore a Cheshire grin, and Greer sobbed.

"If ye have done *anything* to her I'll shove your ballocks down your throat," Elspeth warned, glaring at André.

"Oh no, she is not my type. Too weak." He grinned and winked at Fraser as he referred to Elspeth. "I prefer a woman with a bit of…what is the word? *Bats toi*," he bared his teeth, "*fight* in her."

Fury raged inside him, but Fraser never let André see it. Instead, he kept his face devoid of emotion as he dug his blade into Estienne's throat enough that he drew blood. "Ye would do well to set her aside, André."

The battling continued to roar not only around them but deeper into the woods. Under strict orders to give no quarter, Fraser's men were taking down those heading for the village. If by chance any made it past his men, they may be surprised by what they found.

"As I said, remove your blade and I might just…"

That's all André managed to get out before a blade slammed into his upper thigh and he roared in pain and outrage. The man Fraser and Elspeth had thrown their daggers at the day before grinned and nodded at Fraser.

He had just enough time to nod his acknowledgment before mayhem ensued.

André used Greer as a shield and shoved her at Fraser before his men fell in around him and he began to flee. When Elspeth pursued, Fraser handed Estienne off to the man who had helped them, ordered he be tied to a tree and raced after her.

As a whole, André had accrued more men than he anticipated. That meant more than he would have liked were still left to battle. Which slowed Fraser and Elspeth down enough that the bastard slipped away. But not for long. Not wounded like he was.

His trail would be easy to follow.

He fought by Elspeth's side the entire time, yet again impressed with her skills. It was clear based on the fury on her face that she knew many of the men she cut down. It was also clear that she found a great deal of satisfaction in finally taking revenge on the world she had been thrust into.

As they closed in on the village, she slowed then stopped when she saw what else he had in place. Men dressed as villagers who had been living amongst her kin and people since they relocated here. Ruthless mercenaries all. Which made him wonder how André got his hands on Greer.

"Ye hired them then?" Gratefulness lit Elspeth's eyes as they met his. "Thank ye." She whipped a dagger into a man who rushed her as she kept talking. "They must have cost a fortune!"

They did, but he had managed it. After all, he wasn't known for his cleverness and ability to sniff out treasure for no good reason. Coin was to be had. You just needed to know where to look for it. And men like these were hand-picked and expensive not only because they could fight well but because they would not step out of line in Fraser's absence.

"Why not tell me about them sooner?" She shook her head and dodged a man, letting Fraser have this one as they kept chatting. "To put my mind at ease?"

"Because it could have done the opposite," he pointed out as he snapped the man's neck. "Ye might have worried about why I thought they needed such protection."

"Och, verra true," she allowed and shrugged, tossing him a winning smile before she side kicked one more man then took him down altogether.

Moments later the last of André's men fell.

Elspeth's eyes lingered on Fraser's for a long triumphant moment before she finally turned and raced into her family's waiting arms. The reunion was tearful as Greer joined them followed by the villagers. Though her little sister had been in André's tent, his words proved true. She had not been harmed. She was merely there in case something went wrong.

Apparently, she had been collecting berries and wandered beyond the outskirts of the village without Fraser's mercenaries knowing. One had already lost his life trying to get her back. So it was good that Fraser arrived when he did before more fighting broke out between his men and André. Because talented warriors or not, his mercenaries would have been far outnumbered.

Fraser waited respectfully as Elspeth reunited with her kin but would not linger much longer. He wouldn't risk André getting away for good.

"Audric is standing guard over Estienne," Douglas informed as he and Innis joined him. "Whilst we havenae had time to explore much yet, it seems André has been stockpiling so there's plenty of loot to be had for the men."

"Aye." Innis grinned. "And plenty of whisky as well."

Fraser nodded, pleased. "Tell them to enjoy and take what they like." He gestured at his hired men. "I'll be taking some of them with me to finish André off."

"We're coming too," Douglas said.

"Aye," Innis agreed.

He nodded, understanding well that they wanted vengeance every bit as much as him.

"Will ye be going soon then?" Greer asked, worry in her eyes as she looked to the land behind them. "There are people up that way. Another small village that keeps to themselves." She shook her head. "I dinnae know if André knows about them but 'twill not be good if he does."

Fraser glanced at Douglas and Innis in question, but they only shrugged.

"Many folk come and go in these parts," Innis reminded. "The woodland is thick enough and the hills and caves aplenty so 'tis likely there are villages we dinnae know about." He shook his head. "Hopefully that means André doesnae know of them either."

"Then we should get going." Elspeth blinked away the moisture from reuniting with her kin and stood up a little straighter as she readied for battle once again. Her eyes met Fraser's, and she nodded with determination. "I'm ready to end the bloody bastard once and for all."

He could not agree more. "Aye, then."

Fraser gestured for his men to follow and they headed out. As he knew would be the case, it wasn't long before they picked up a blood trail. Better yet, several trails.

"He's trying to throw us off his tracks," Fraser muttered as he ordered everyone to split up.

"We should go that way." Elspeth pointed in a direction that was steeper than the others. "He would go the least obvious route." Her eyes narrowed. "And he might just be inclined to follow that plume of smoke I see up there."

He agreed as he caught sight of it. If there were vulnerable people about he would use them as either a human shield or a bargaining chip. So they started in that direction. At first, it was simple enough but soon became more of a challenge as the way steepened.

"I'll go first," Elspeth declared.

"Ye will do no such thing," Fraser argued.

"I will. I *must*." Her eyes widened. "Did ye not know I'm afraid of heights and climbing isnae my strongpoint?" She looked at Douglas. "Go on. Tell him." Her eyes shot back to Fraser. "So I would feel much safer with ye behind me to catch me if need be."

He turned narrowed eyes her brother's way. "Is it true then? Does she fear heights?"

Douglas frowned. "I didnae think so."

"How little ye remember then, Brother!" She shook her head. "We havenae time for this."

She set off without a backward glance, leaving no room for further argument. He sighed and followed, hoping for the best. Just as he knew would happen, certain areas grew more perilous and far thicker with spruces, birches, and shrubs. And just as he forecasted, those areas stole Elspeth from his sight. Though the moments were brief and they moved swiftly, it still left him uneasy. She was more vulnerable than he would like.

"It seems ye climb just fine, after all, lass," he muttered as he joined her on a ledge and eyed the next small climb. "I dinnae like this."

"'Twill be fine," Elspeth assured. "And just look," she continued innocently as she tied her hair back more securely with the bandana. "It seems climbing comes more naturally to me than it once did." She shook her head, quite sure of herself. "So dinnae worry. I'll be careful and keep my eyes open."

"'Tis a merry chase the bastard's giving us, aye?" Douglas grumbled as he joined them and peered up. "It looks like we're nearly to the top."

Fraser eyed their surroundings, somewhat familiar with the area. "André definitely chose the most difficult route."

"Aye," Douglas agreed. "Which means he must be tiring."

"That's right," Elspeth agreed as she grabbed a bush root and started up the next incline.

"Och, and where's that fear of heights she claims to have had?" Fraser muttered as he pursued her. He knew what she was up to.

She wanted to catch up with André first.

However understandable her reasoning, she was letting her vengeance get the better of her. Because the enemy did just what Fraser figured he might. Or so he assumed when moments after she vanished up the next bend, a dagger whipped by his face.

"Bloody hell," he growled, gesturing that Douglas hold back as he assessed the situation.

That meant becoming more vulnerable as he hoisted himself up the rest of the way. No sooner did he make it to the top when another blade whipped his way. He dodged it then leapt to his feet moments before a man rushed him.

The two came together near the edge and teetered for a moment before Fraser got the upper hand and drove him back. Meanwhile, Douglas scrambled up and started battling another. If he were to guess based on their skills, these were some of André's best men.

Four of them to be precise. Two were after him and the other two Douglas.

The battling was fast and vicious, but at least they were holding their own. Yet as he fought, a knot of dread formed in the pit of his stomach. There was no sign of Elspeth. Where was she? Was she all right? Moments later, a breath away from driving his blade through his opponent's gut, his question was answered.

"If you kill my men," came André's dark, threatening voice, "I *will* kill Elspeth."

Shaking with rage, Fraser pulled his blade back when André dragged Elspeth into the clearing. Remarkably calm, her resolved eyes met Fraser's. She knew she had rushed into this. That her long hatred of the man had blinded her to logical thinking. But who could blame her? André had ruined her life in so many ways.

"Dinnae listen to him, Fraser." Her fearless eyes narrowed. "Finish off his men then end him." She both challenged and begged him. "Do it for me."

It would not happen. He would never give her up. Not for anything.

"Nay." He shook his head. "I willnae let ye sacrifice yourself."

Because that is exactly what she offered to do.

He swiftly took in the entirety of the situation. Though he could take down the men that stood in his way, it would still allow enough time for the enemy to swipe his blade. Then there was always the chance he could get a dagger into André, but with the wind shear, it was risky. He might hit Elspeth. Worse yet, André might jerk his knife in reflex and kill her.

When André pressed the blade tighter, Fraser looked at Douglas and shook his head. They had no choice. He had not come all this way for her to be taken away from him now. Her life was far too important.

They had to surrender.

Though Douglas hesitated for a moment, his need to end the enemy substantial, he, at last, nodded in agreement and they tossed aside their blades.

"Ballocks, no," Elspeth whispered as a wide smile started to split André's face.

A smile, as it turned out, that soon turned to shock when a perfectly aimed arrow suddenly ripped through his neck.

Fraser wasted no time but took advantage of André's men's momentary confusion and opened their throats with one efficient swipe of his sword. Douglas moved swiftly as well and handled the other two.

As they fell, Fraser glanced up at the ledge to see who their silent hero was.

Who he saw there, however, was most certainly the last person he ever expected.

Chapter Sixteen

THE MOMENT THE arrow hit André, Elspeth spun and knocked his blade free. A blink later, Fraser's dagger hit his sword arm as he fell to his knees. Now he was utterly useless. In a position she had long dreamed he would be.

Time slowed.

This was her moment.

The end of so much torment.

Blood trickled out of the corner of his mouth as he gurgled something indiscernible. She didn't care what it was. His words were pointless. Not worth hearing. Never to be heard again. The sound of fighting behind her faded away as she stared down at him with frigid indifference.

As she recalled all the harm he had done.

He might not have been there that fateful night years ago, but it was his orders that resulted in so much death. The loss of her kin. The loss of a life that had meant so much to her. She cared nothing for the physical suffering she had endured at his hands, but what he'd done to those she loved.

"This is for them," she growled, a venomous bite to her voice. "For the villagers that lost their lives both times." She leaned close and narrowed her eyes. "And most especially for my husband and daughter."

As slowly and painfully as possible, she dragged her blade across his throat then stepped back as he finally fell to his death. She stared at him, relishing the moment for all it was worth. Wishing it could go on for far longer.

When Fraser's gentle hand landed on her shoulder, her eyes drifted to his.

"Look, lass," he murmured.

Her eyes followed his to where the arrow had come from.

A girl perhaps a few years older than Greer aimed an arrow at Douglas as she glanced nervously between him and Fraser. Yet her curious eyes went to Elspeth as well.

Eyes that matched her own.

Features so very similar.

Elspeth blinked several times. It could not be, could it? Was she seeing clearly?

"Aileann?" she said hoarsely, sure she must be seeing a ghost. "Is that *ye*, Daughter?"

She had died. That had been confirmed.

Or so she thought.

"Who are ye?" The girl's eyes narrowed as she shifted her aim to Fraser. "Speak now, or he dies next."

"My name is Elspeth MacLauchlin." She ignored the tear that rolled down her cheek. What if she were wrong? What if she only saw what she wanted to see? She began inwardly praying as she continued talking. "I once had a daughter that looked just like ye. She was taken from me when she was a wee lassie…taken from a small village on the eastern shores of Scotland."

"MacLauchlin," the girl murmured. Her arrow remained notched, but the intense look in her eyes lessened. "Why are ye here?"

Though tempted to keep questioning her she got the sense the girl would have her answers first. That she possessed an overly cautious nature and a stubborn disposition. Two personality traits she more than understood and respected.

"I'm here..." Elspeth gestured at Fraser and Douglas. "*We're* here to protect my people and kin from the man ye just killed." She pointed back the way they had come. "They live down there but once resided on the eastern shores of Scotland." She cocked her head. "Might I tell ye our story, child? Might I share?"

The girl considered her for several moments. Her every feature bespoke the little girl she had lost all those years ago. The same sparkling eyes. The same curly hair.

"Aye, ye can share," the girl finally responded.

So she did, recounting everything that had happened that fateful night.

"I called to ye over and over," she managed in closure, her voice thick with emotion. "I said Aileann MacLauchlin, ye stay strong." She shook her head and wiped away another tear, lost in the horrific memory. "I called out to ye to always stay verra strong no matter what."

Silence fell as her words lingered. As she continued to pray. Please let this be her. Not a desperate mother's misguided mirage of hope.

Let her say what I want to hear. Let this be real.

At long last, the girl finally spoke. And thankfully, by the grace of God, her every word tore away the years. Every syllable marked the closure of an unending nightmare.

"Aye," she whispered as she slowly lowered the bow, her voice wobbly. "And I did...I stayed strong." Her eyes remained with Elspeth's. "'Twas that voice in the night, *your* voice, that got me through ever since."

Elspeth nodded as more tears fell, muted for a moment as her daughter's words truly sunk in.

"I'm so verra glad," she finally managed softly. "Because 'twas your memory that did the same for me."

Though Aileann had lowered her bow and closed the distance, she still kept a wary eye on the men.

"God above 'tis really ye," Elspeth whispered as her daughter stopped in front of her. "'Tis really truly ye."

Now that she was close, she could see the moisture in the girl's eyes. The sharp intelligence. More than that, mayhap recognition.

"I was told my parents died," Aileann murmured. "Yet here ye stand…the lass from my dreams…"

"Your da did die," she said sadly. "But not me, lassie. Not your ma," she whispered. "I didnae die and stand before ye now."

The moment stretched as her daughter considered her before she finally murmured, "I do…I remember ye." Though strength remained in her steady gaze, the vulnerable little girl was in there too. The fear and long, lonely years. "I remember ye, Ma."

Based on the tears in her eyes, she truly did. She remembered.

"I'm so glad to hear it, Aileann," was all Elspeth was capable of saying before she pulled her daughter into her arms and held on tight. Tears fell, but she barely felt them. All she could feel was her baby girl back in her arms. A long lost dream come true.

"Those that took me called me Ceit, but now I am Cullodena," the girl said softly, emotion obvious in her voice as they embraced. "We all took new names when we began our lives here."

Though she never wanted to let her go, Elspeth finally pulled back and wiped away her tears. "Cullodena is a verra bonny name." She offered a warm smile as she brushed a tear from her daughter's cheek. "Did ye pick it yourself?"

"Aye," she replied. "For the broken mossy land I so enjoy."

Though Elspeth had many questions, endless questions, she would wait rather than overwhelm her.

"I would like to see this mossy land." She kept smiling. "And I would like to meet your people."

She proceeded to introduce Fraser and Douglas, who, as it happened, Cullodena had known from afar.

"'Tis so good to see ye again, Niece." Douglas embraced her, his emotion evident. "Ye were sorely missed."

Cullodena only nodded, her eyes lingering on him before her attention returned to the shore. "Ye got them all, aye? André's pirates that were making this land their own?"

"Ye knew his name then?" Elspeth said, surprised.

"Aye," she confirmed. "I have watched all the comings and goings around here for years." Her eyes went to Fraser. "From Captain MacLomain with the lass carved into his prow to the other pirates roaming these shores."

She could tell by the way her daughter looked from Fraser to her that she recognized the woman on the prow as Elspeth. She also realized, much to her shock, that her daughter did not particularly fear pirates.

"Aye, we killed all of André's men," Elspeth replied to Cullodena's question. "His crew are gone now." She looked at her curiously as she gestured to the dying fire nearby. "Did ye light that?" Her daughter was no doubt a clever girl if not a risk-taker. And she had made it clear she watched everything closely. Perhaps even the battle they just fought and who might have survived it. "Mayhap ye lit it on purpose to lure André this way?"

"I did light it." Cullodena nodded. "And aye, 'twas to lure him this way." Her look was very matter-of-fact and her tone nowhere near sorry. "I saw an opportunity, and I took it." She frowned at André's broken body. "I've seen what this man is capable of."

"'Twas verra dangerous for ye to do," Elspeth murmured. "Ye could have been hurt."

"But I wasnae." Her eyes returned to Elspeth. "Nor were ye."

"Och," she began, but Fraser came to her daughter's rescue and spoke first. "Ye cannae fault the lassie for being so much like her mother, aye?" He winked at Elspeth. "Courageous if not trying at times."

She supposed he had her there.

Cullodena's eyes went from Fraser to his ships bobbing in the harbor. "Though I didnae trust getting too close, I always knew 'twas a good thing when those ships arrived." Her eyes went to his. "That ye were seeing to your people."

"Your people, lass," he said softly. "They are verra much your kin."

"Fraser and his men are friends, not foe," Elspeth assured before she explained all he had done for them before they arrived on these shores. "We are here to protect and help ye and yours any way we can."

Cullodena's sharp eyes returned to Fraser. "Yet many pirates come here for other reasons."

Fraser's brows swept up at her vague implication. "Such as?"

"I think ye know." Her eyes went from Douglas to Elspeth. "I think ye all know."

It seemed her daughter was knowledgeable about her kin's history.

"Ye know about it, aye?" Elspeth murmured. "Ye have heard of the MacLauchlin treasure."

"Verra few in these parts havenae." Cullodena watched them closely. "So are ye here for treasure too then?"

Elspeth met Fraser's eyes before she looked at her daughter again. It was time to come clean. So she urged her to sit on a rock beside her then shared everything from the very beginning. She left nothing out. From she and Fraser falling in love to her kidnapping, then the years since.

After she finished, Cullodena eyed Fraser for a long moment. "So ye became something ye disliked so much to find my mother?" Her eyes drifted to his ship again as she whispered, "I heard tale that ye sought to avenge the lass that sat on your prow and I always wondered who she was. What sort of person inspired such passion."

"Now ye know," Fraser murmured. "I would have become a pirate several times over to save your ma."

She nodded, as her eyes returned to him then took in Elspeth's outfit with a small smile. "It seems many have embraced the ways of a pirate to see justice served." Her eyes fell to André whose blank, lifeless eyes stared at the sky. "To see men the likes of him no more."

"Aye," Elspeth agreed. "He is but part of your past now, lassie."

"Good." Cullodena gave him one last disgusted look. "I am verra happy I was part of his demise." Her eyes met Elspeth's. "For all he has done to us and our kin."

"Aye, my lass." She nodded. "And whilst I dinnae like ye putting yourself in harm's way, I'm thankful for your brave actions." Pride lit her eyes as she gazed at her daughter. "Ye are *verra* talented with the bow."

Her daughter grinned. "Thank ye."

Confident enough that their reunion was going well, curiosity won over, and she asked a few more questions.

"How did ye end up here, Cullodena? So far from your original home?" She shook her head, baffled. "How did ye end up on what was once MacLauchlin land?"

So she told them.

Apparently, one of Estienne's men had snagged her to give to a lass he was wooing. A woman desperate for a child of her own. By the sounds of it, though not right in the head, she had not mistreated Cullodena. Still, her daughter led a poor life surrounded by vagrant pirates that came and went. A life where she needed to learn to fight and protect herself if she hoped to survive.

"The lass who called herself my ma protected me the best she could but 'twas still wise to be on guard," Cullodena explained. "When sickness came to the village, and she died, I knew I couldnae stay on any longer." She shook her head. "So I gathered up those who wished to travel with me and headed this way. The MacLauchlin name was all I had to follow thanks to your words that night."

Thank the good Lord she had said them then.

"Did the woman who called herself your mother have a sister?" Elspeth asked, thinking back on André's wench and her assurance that Elspeth's child was dead.

"Aye, actually," she replied. "A coarse woman with a sympathetic heart in the end."

When Elspeth looked at her in question, she continued. "She never seemed to have much use for me but before I fled she embraced me and told me to be strong just like ye had. She said I had a chance at a new life. She swore she would say I was dead." She shook her head. "No matter who asked or who they said they were." She kept shaking her head. "'Cause no one was to be trusted."

Elspeth nodded, never more grateful to anyone in her life than she was to that woman. Some mothers might get angry that they weren't told their daughter was alive but she knew better. She understood the life of pirates and most especially the tyrant André had been. Had he found out about Cullodena everything might have gone very differently.

"Well I'm grateful she looked after you in the end," Elspeth said softly, brushing a lock of hair from her daughter's forehead like she used to when she was little. "It must have been quite the journey across Scotland for ye."

"'Twas not so bad," Cullodena said. "I've always been good in the woodland and know how to survive."

"Just like your great-great grandmother who first led our ancestors to the east coast," she murmured as she embraced her again, so grateful to have found her. It was a miracle she had survived. A blessing, actually, that she had not suffered a far worse fate. But then it seemed she had angels along the way.

"Might I meet your people?" Elspeth asked as she pulled back. "Might I see where ye have been living?"

When Cullodena hesitated, her eyes flickering back to Fraser, he said, "I will stay behind if 'twould make ye more comfortable, lass."

Wise beyond her years, she eyed him for another moment before she shook her head. "Nay, ye are a different sort, Fraser MacLomain." Her eyes flickered from Elspeth back to him. "The sort I'd be glad to call kin."

Elspeth could tell by the relieved look in Fraser's eyes when he nodded, that her words meant a lot. They meant a lot to her as well.

Her daughter stood, and whistled, the sound almost identical to a bird. Moments later, having been in hiding, a few people appeared through the woods. Cullodena made brief introductions before she took the newcomers aside, spoke softly then returned to Elspeth.

"My friends have agreed to welcome all of ye." She started into the forest. "Follow me."

They remained in the woods for a short time before they entered a cave that seemed to wrap back the way they had come. Though not as steep, they proceeded to go downhill through a mix of wider caverns and smaller tunnels. Essentially, they were heading for the shore again. Where they came out was cushioned by cliffs and remote enough that it was hidden from the ocean.

"I know this place," Fraser commented as his eyes went to a waterfall off to their right. "I came here often as a child."

"Aye then?" She grinned and teased him. "And just think ye might have been close to a long lost treasure."

"Aye," he murmured as he took her hand and looked at her with adoration. "Treasure now found."

Warmed by the affectionate light in his eyes, she was about to respond but stopped short as a small community of people appeared.

"Am I seeing correctly?" she said softly, not referring to the people.

"Ye are," Fraser murmured as they stared at a stone peeking out of a flat overgrown area. A rock the exact color of Elspeth's stones. A rock they realized sat on what must be an old foundation.

They smiled as their eyes met.

Against the odds, they had found what they were looking for.

They had arrived at the ruins of MacLauchlin Castle.

Chapter Seventeen

A s it turned out, Cullodena and the handful of people traveling with her had made their homes in the various caves around the castle ruins. In truth, Fraser was amazed they had not been discovered up to this point. It spoke to their discretion and cunning.

Yet despite their cautionary way of living, they proved more receptive to welcoming him and Elspeth than he expected. But then, as they soon discovered, their love tale was now legendary. As was how he once saved a small village on the eastern shores of Scotland.

So Cullodena had known this all along. Who he was. That he could be trusted. Yet she still felt him out. Just as she did now while they sat together around a small fire. "What would ye do if ye found the MacLauchlin treasure, Captain MacLomain?"

He didn't have to consider that long.

"I would see enough go to the crew of *The Sea Hellions* for fighting on behalf of Elspeth and me," he replied. "Then the rest would go to protecting ye and your people. *All* of your people." He eyed their surroundings. "Mayhap by rebuilding your castle here or closer to my kin."

"Are your kin pirates like ye then?" she asked.

"Not nearly." He chuckled. "But they are verra powerful and good allies to have."

"Do ye miss them?"

"Aye." His eyes went to Elspeth. "But I'll see them again soon enough."

"So ye'll be leaving us then?" Cullodena's gaze fell to Elspeth's ring. "When 'tis clear ye are set to marry my ma."

"I will be wherever she is," he assured, squeezing his lass's hand. "Which I imagine will be both places on different occasions."

He could tell by the warmth in Elspeth's eyes that she liked the sound of that. He also saw that she was finally ready to see if there was anything to be found at the end of a longstanding family vendetta.

"Might I use the stones then, Daughter?" Love shone in Elspeth's eyes as they turned back to her daughter. "Might we at long last see where they lead?… if they lead to anything at all?"

Cullodena looked back and forth between her and Fraser before her eyes went to her people. "What say ye, friends? And consider carefully. Because if they find something, our lives will change forever."

The girl closest to her leaned over and squeezed her hand. "I think it already has." She looked at Fraser and Elspeth. "For the better." Then her eyes returned to Cullodena. "I think some part of ye always hoped the treasure might bring kin your way…that some good might come from that terrible night ye lost them."

Cullodena's eyes grew moist before she nodded then looked Fraser and Elspeth's way. "Aye, then."

Elspeth smiled at her daughter before she looked at the sky. The sun was just beginning to set, but a bright star in the north was already visible. That had to be it. So she lined up the stones on the castle ruins just as she had on his desk. Almost immediately they saw the landmarks pieced together by the marks. The jagged archway below the star, then what lay beyond.

"A stretch of broken mossy land," Elspeth whispered as her eyes went to her daughter's. "Just like your name…your favorite spot."

"Aye," Cullodena said softly as she urged them to follow her in that direction.

On the other side of the archway, they found a unique spot vulnerable to the elements. A waterfall poured down a sheet of rock into a muddied pool tucked back under a wedge of mossy rock. Bereft of sunlight, the only thing the area offered was a vantage point of the ocean that he knew would be hidden from ships. All and all, it was by no means a spot he would think a young girl would enjoy let alone favor so highly that she named herself after it.

But then, like her mother, Cullodena was no average lass.

A fact she soon proved.

"I have stood here often and watched the sea," she murmured, nostalgic. "I always knew that it would be a pirate that reconnected me with what I lost so long ago." Her eyes went to Elspeth. "That it would be the verra beast who stole my life that would someday return it to me." Her voice softened. "Or should I say 'twas a hero who returned it to me."

Cullodena turned to Fraser. "Thank ye for that, Captain MacLomain." Her eyes grew moist. "Thank ye for loving my ma so well and for seeing to my kin when ye didnae have to." Her eyes went to the waterfall. "Ye have verra much earned your prize."

Curious, he glanced from the waterfall back to her before he headed that way.

Between the muddy water, frothing bubbles and lack of light, it was hard to see anything of consequence. Or so he thought until Cullodena joined him and proved otherwise with a T shaped contraption. She leaned over, dug down in and raked forward before she stuck her hand in, felt around then lifted something out.

"Bloody hell," he whispered as she handed him a solid gold bar. "The treasure actually exists!"

"There is far more down there," she informed, grinning at his dumbfounded expression. "Plus jewels."

He shook his head before he finally met her grin then smiled at Elspeth, only one thought on his mind. "By the sounds of it, there's more than enough to protect ye and yours for several lifetimes."

Many hours and a family reunion later, he remained in awe as he and Elspeth sat alone on the shore just beyond the ruins of MacLauchlin Castle. Cullodena had finally met her people, and they spent a truly wonderful evening reconnecting. She was already fast friends with Greer and Arabel and had spent ample time bonding with Elspeth, who still beamed with happiness.

Having been given several gold bars in addition to André's loot and ships, *The Sea Hellions* were celebrating too just in a separate location for the moment. Best to keep pirates and villagers apart for this period of adjustment. Well, all but Innis, Audric, and Douglas, of course.

Fiddles still played in the distance as people danced, laughed and had a merry good time.

"Was it me or was Audric eying my Cullodena?" she grumbled, her eyes narrowed as she contemplated it. "She's but a child!"

"A child on the brink of womanhood," he reminded gently though he couldn't help a grin and shrug. "Ye cannae overly blame the lad. Not only is she independent and full of fire, but possesses the same bonny looks as her ma."

"She *is* verra bonny, isnae she?" She sighed and relented. "And I suppose a wee bit fiery and independent."

He arched his brows and kept grinning. "Just a *wee* bit?"

"Aye, just a wee bit and no more," she muttered, in complete denial. It would be interesting watching the two of them together over the years. Very entertaining he imagined.

Speaking of entertaining.

He could think of far better things to do right now than talk.

Yet it seemed more weighed on her mind.

"Do ye think Audric did it then?" she murmured as he peppered kisses down her neck. "Do ye think he ended Estienne?"

According to Magnus, he had been found tied to a tree with his throat slit. And they both knew her former apprentice had been tasked with keeping an eye on him.

"'Tis hard to know," he replied as he inhaled her sweet scent. "Though I wouldnae blame him if he did."

"Nor I," she whispered after his lips brushed hers. "In fact, it seems fitting that Audric be the one to do it. That he ended the son of the man that had used him. That he saw an end to the tainted blood in his family."

"Aye," he agreed, kissing her again.

"And what will ye do with the journal Magnus found?" she murmured. "André's book full of the comings and goings of the French navy and their privateers?"

"Likely hand it over to Shaw," he replied. "As a show of good faith."

"'Tis quite the show of faith," she commented though he saw the approval in her eyes.

"Aye," he agreed. "But worth the extra good favor if we remain in the area." He gave her a pointed look. "If we remain so close to his stronghold in Scarba."

"Verra true," she murmured around a kiss before meeting his eyes again. "So what now, Fraser? Will we stay here or go see your kin? Will we settle or live the lives of pirates?"

His eyes went to his ship and lingered. He had often thought when this was all over he would head home and never look back. But now, as he had implied to her daughter, he saw a different sort of life ahead. One that didn't just include his kin but her people and the sea he had come to love.

The adventure he had come to crave.

"What do ye see ahead for us, lass?" He couldn't help a knowing smile as his eyes returned to hers. "In between giving Culladena at least two brothers and a sister, of course."

"Och!" Her eyes widened in unmistakable pleasure. "Ye see us having that many wee ones, aye?" Then her eyes narrowed. "Is this your gift of foresight talking, then?"

"Aye." Because it was. "We have a verra full and good life ahead of us, my wee lassie."

She looked to his ship then back at him, a smile hovering on her lips. "Then I say we do just that." The corner of her mouth shot up in a devious grin. "I say we live it to the fullest, Cap'n MacLomain."

In complete agreement, he lowered her to the blanket and began doing that very thing.

Though he had traveled a winding sometimes dark path since he first washed up on Elspeth's shore over two winters ago, he would do it all again.

Anything to have her in his arms where she belonged.

Anything to at last live life together.

As it would be told for many generations to come, a roguish MacLomain pirate known as the Robin Hood of the seas, found far more than good fortune in the end. Far more than just gold and wealth beyond his wildest imagination.

He discovered *real* treasure.

The best sort really.

Long lost kin, and an untouchable love with his beloved wife, Elspeth MacLauchlin.

More than that?

An unforgettable lifetime of adventure, mischief, and mayhem with his wee pirate lassie.

THE END

About the Author

Sky Purington is the bestselling author of nearly forty novels and novellas. A New Englander born and bred who recently moved to Virginia, Sky was raised hearing stories of folklore, myth, and legend. When combined with a love for history, romance, and time-travel, elements from the stories of her youth found release in her books.

Purington loves to hear from readers and can be contacted at Sky@SkyPurington.com. Interested in keeping up with Sky's latest news and releases? Either visit Sky's website, www.SkyPurington.com, join her quarterly newsletter, or sign up for personalized text message alerts. Simply text 'skypurington' (no quotes, one word, all lowercase) to 74121 or visit Sky's Sign-up Page. Texts will ONLY be sent when there is a new book release. Readers can easily opt out at any time.

Facebook: facebook.com/sky.purington
Twitter: twitter.com/skypurington
BookBub: bookbub.com/authors/sky-purington
Pinterest: pinterest.com/skypurington

Also by Sky Purington

~The MacLomain Series – Early Years~
Highland Defiance – Book One
Highland Persuasion – Book Two
Highland Mystic – Book Three

~The MacLomain Series~
The King's Druidess – Prelude
Fate's Monolith – Book One
Destiny's Denial – Book Two
Sylvan Mist – Book Three

~The MacLomain Series – Next Generation~
Mark of the Highlander – Book One
Vow of the Highlander – Book Two
Wrath of the Highlander – Book Three
Faith of the Highlander – Book Four
Plight of the Highlander – Book Five

~The MacLomain Series – Viking Ancestors~
Viking King – Book One
Viking Claim – Book Two
Viking Heart – Book Three

~The MacLomain Series – Later Years~
Quest of a Scottish Warrior – Book One
Yule's Fallen Angel – Spin-off Novella
Honor of a Scottish Warrior – Book Two
Oath of a Scottish Warrior – Book Three
Passion of a Scottish Warrior – Book Four

~The MacLomain Series – Viking Ancestors' Kin~

Rise of a Viking – Book One

Vengeance of a Viking – Book Two

A Viking Holiday – Spin-off Novella, Book 2.5

Soul of a Viking – Book Three

Fury of a Viking – Book Four

Destiny's Dragon – Spin-off Novella, Book 4.5

Pride of a Viking – Book Five

~The MacLomain Series: A New Beginning~

Sworn to a Highland Laird – Book One

Taken by a Highland Laird – Book Two

Promised to a Highland Laird – Book Three

Avenged by a Highland Laird – Book Four

~Pirates of Britannia World~

The Seafaring Rogue

The MacLomain Series: A New Beginning Spin-off

~Viking Ancestors: Rise of the Dragon~

Viking King's Vendetta – Book One

Viking's Valor – Book Two

Viking's Intent – Book Three

Viking's Ransom – Book Four

Viking's Conquest – Book Five

Viking's Crusade – Book Six

~Calum's Curse Series~

The Victorian Lure – Book One

The Georgian Embrace – Book Two

The Tudor Revival – Book Three

Made in the USA
Middletown, DE
17 July 2019